Emma and the Love Spell

Emma and the Love Spell

Meredith Ireland

BLOOMSBURY
CHILDREN'S BOOKS
NEW YORK LONDON OXFORD NEW DELHI SYDNEY

For my heart and my sunshine and
anyone with a little magic in them

BLOOMSBURY CHILDREN'S BOOKS
Bloomsbury Publishing Inc., part of Bloomsbury Publishing Plc
1385 Broadway, New York, NY 10018

First published in the United States of America in January 2024 by Bloomsbury Children's Books

Bloomsbury books may be purchased for business or promotional use. For information on bulk purchases please contact Macmillan Corporate and Premium Sales Department at specialmarkets@macmillan.com

Library of Congress Cataloging-in-Publication Data
available upon request
ISBN 978-1-5476-1260-4 (hardcover) • ISBN 978-1-5476-1261-1 (e-book)

Book design by Yelena Safronova
Typeset by Westchester Publishing Services
Printed and bound in the U.S.A.
2 4 6 8 10 9 7 5 3 1

To find out more about our authors and books visit www.bloomsbury.com
and sign up for our newsletters.

1

It was a perfect Thursday afternoon. One of those June days where it was hot but not as we walked barefoot through the creek. Our ice cream had dripped in the sun, but it was goose-bumps cold in the shade. The air smelled like sunscreen and wildflowers. And the dusting of freckles on Avangeline's cheeks had started to show like the stars at night.

My best friend and I shared a towel on a grassy slope by the Keeble River. Sixth grade had just ended, and I had all kinds of plans for us.

Emma Davidson's Plan for an Epic Summer with Avangeline Monroe:

1. Adventure every day in the woods

2. Eat wild raspberries until our lips are stained
3. Ride our bikes until our legs hurt
4. Pound slushies without getting brain freeze
5. Stay up late watching movies every Friday night
6. Have three sleepovers a week

It was going to be awesome.

I lay back, shading my eyes with my hand, but Avangeline sat holding her knees. She'd been a little quiet on the ride over and a lot quiet by the river.

"Whatcha thinking?" I asked.

She stared ahead, hazel eyes glued to the water below us. The Keeble was deep in parts, especially as it ran under Holy Cross Bridge, but here it was only about knee high.

When Avangeline stayed quiet, I sat up too. Next to each other, we looked like opposites. She had curls that got blonder in the sun, and my straight strands never changed. I'd always thought of my hair as plain black, but she said it was like onyx—her favorite gemstone.

We'd been best friends since I'd moved to town. We even had matching woven bracelets to prove it. Avangeline was my first friend in Samsonville and also kind of my only friend.

"Hey, you okay?" I asked.

"Oh, yeah, sorry." She had a slightly lopsided smile,

the right end higher than the left. I liked it. It was part of what made her Avangeline.

"What's on your mind?"

She sighed. "A lot."

Insects sang their summer song, and I swore they got louder bit by bit—what our chorus teacher called a "crescendo." Avangeline could name every bug just from its noise. She loved animals and nature. I did too, but my relationship with them was . . . complicated.

"You know you can tell me anything, right?" I said.

She turned toward me, stretching her tan legs out in front of her. Avangeline's skin bronzed in the summer. Meanwhile, I stayed Kpop pale.

She frowned. "I know, Emmie. It's just . . . I don't know how to say this. And I don't want to. Because if I tell you, it's real."

A sinking feeling hit my core, like I was in an elevator that was dropping too fast. What didn't she want to say? What secrets could she be keeping from me?

Clouds rushed into the sky, blotting out the bright sun. Something was coming. Something bad. I gripped the towel and held my breath.

"It's my mom and dad." She broke off a long piece of grass and tore it apart. "They . . . they say they're not in love anymore."

"Oh Lina, I'm so sorry," I said.

She hated the nickname Ava, so we'd come up with

Lina a while ago. Mostly, though, I called her Avangeline, because I loved how all the syllables felt on my tongue.

"Yeah." She tossed the grass pieces aside.

We sat in silence. I didn't know what to say or how to make it better. Breakups happened all the time in school. People said they were in love on a Tuesday, and then by Friday they were done. Avangeline had dated James Witten for a super-long sixteen days over the winter before dumping him, but we were in sixth grade. I didn't understand how adults suddenly fell out of love. Not when they had kids. Avangeline's little brother, Max, was only six. Now what would happen? They'd probably have to split time between two houses like Jackson Tacetta. His parents got divorced last year, and after that his dad picked him up every other Wednesday in a shiny yellow convertible.

Avangeline's face was stormy, her brown eyebrows turned up in the center. Anger bubbled up inside me at seeing her upset. The storm clouds overhead swirled, and . . . I needed to get a grip. Immediately.

I closed my eyes and exhaled slowly.

Calm down, Emma. Don't jump to conclusions. Everything might be okay. They could be like Isabella Miles's parents, who hated each other and were always fighting but stayed together. Falling out of love didn't mean things *had to* change.

I chased the dark thoughts away, and the sunlight returned.

Luckily, Avangeline was looking down at her toe rings, too lost in thought to notice the rapid changes in the sky.

"So, what's going to happen?" I asked.

Avangeline's jaw ticked like she was chewing gum. "They want to get divorced."

I threw my arms around her shoulders, hugging her. She smelled like baby powder and crisp apples, as always. She leaned her head on my shoulder.

"There's more." She took a deep breath, her chest rising. "My mom wants to move back to Louisiana, where she grew up. Grandma Lulu, Aunt Hannah, and my cousins still live down there, and Grandma has a big house she needs help with anyhow."

"Lina," I gasped. Her relationship with her mom was complicated, since her mom was bossy and Lina definitely wasn't, but having her mom that far away was going to be super hard. But maybe she'd just spend more time at my house. Mom and Dad were pretty great, and they were always happy to have her over.

"It'll be okay," I said.

She shook her head. "It won't. She's taking me and Max with her. The three of us are moving to New Orleans."

She finally looked me in the eye. Her long brown

lashes were wet, and her mood ring had turned black, and it was like the world had cracked in two. I blinked hard, trying to shuffle everything back into place. But Avangeline had just said she was leaving Samsonville for good. She was going all the way to Louisiana to stay there. Her family went once a year to visit, but she always came back.

This time she wouldn't.

I shook my head. I couldn't have heard her right. But the knots in my stomach said otherwise.

"When?" I croaked out, my mouth suddenly dry.

"In a month. Mom wants us to 'get settled in' before school starts in August."

I shook my head again, my long hair waving. It was impossible. This couldn't be happening. I grabbed her hand. "But you can't go."

She drew in a sharp breath and squeezed my fingers. "I know, but I have to, Emmie. They already decided. I can't stay here with Dad because he travels for work and I'm 'only twelve' and that's 'too young to be alone.' I said I could handle it, and Dad agreed, but . . . you know how my mom is. She doesn't really listen to me. Plus, Max will go with Mom no matter what, and if I stay, I wouldn't see him. I've asked if we can come back for visits, but Dad said he'd come down when he could, and Mom thinks we should have a 'fresh start,' so . . ."

Avangeline trailed off, and I filled in the blanks in my head.

So . . . I'd never see her again.

So . . . our lives as we knew them were ending.

So . . . we wouldn't be best friends anymore.

It would be like my classmates in Boston, who'd all promised to keep in touch before I moved. Some of them did for a little while, but then it was kind of "out of sight, out of mind." It's not the same if you can't hang out or be there when something happens in class. They made new friends, I made a new friend, and that was it. And it hadn't bothered me because I'd never been as close with any of them as I was with Avangeline.

Only now I'd lose her too.

I bit my lower lip until it hurt.

I tried. I promise I did.

With my eyes shut, I took breaths so deep my chest felt like a balloon about to pop. I tried to turn off my brain and ignore everything but the rush of air coming into and leaving my lungs. To feel nothing but the plush towel under my palms. To remain calm and listen to the insects. I really tried.

But they'd stopped singing.

In the quiet it felt like pressure clamping onto my heart and chaos swirling in my chest. All of it wanted to come out. Now.

My eyes shot open. *Oh no. No. Not here. Not now. Anything but this.*

My hands shook as I tried to contain it, but the power, the *feeling* was like a tidal wave cresting way above my head and just as scary. But I couldn't allow myself to feel scared. Or happy. Or sad. Or anything other than calm. I had to stay neutral and act normal like my parents always told me to. No matter what.

But I couldn't fake it, because Avangeline was going to leave. I'd never see her again.

I lost control.

Energy shot through me, and for a second it felt great. Like breaking the surface after staying underwater for too long. But then slate-gray storm clouds rolled in faster than I'd ever seen. Wind whipped around Avangeline's curls, and thunder clapped above us. Electricity sizzled in my blood, like little tingles running up and down my arms.

No. No. No.

Please stop. Go away.

I couldn't do this in front of her. Heat and shame flooded me. I breathed quickly, trying to make the feeling end, but I was too late.

No. No. No.

"Oh wow, I didn't think it was supposed to rain today," Lina said.

She barely got the words out before a bolt of lightning streaked across the dark sky. It was brilliant and jagged as it struck the river. Then fat raindrops fell. Just a couple of splatters first, before it poured like someone had turned on a garden hose.

We scrambled to gather our things and hopped on our bikes. I needed to get out of there. Immediately.

"Are you coming back to my house?" Avangeline asked.

"No, I . . . I left stuff out in my yard. I have to bring it in," I said, searching for a lie. "See ya."

I took off before Avangeline could say anything else. I was plain lucky she hadn't noticed that my magic had drained all the color out of our towel.

It had also struck the Keeble with lightning, but I mean . . . she'd noticed that part. She just hadn't known I'd done it. Well, my powers had.

I really hoped nothing was hurt in the river, but I couldn't stop to check. I needed to get home, get this cursed magic under control, and end the storm.

2

I wasn't always powerful.

Or magical.

Or whatever the heck this was.

I was a normal baby born in Korea. My parents adopted me when I was four months old, and for most of my life, we lived in Boston, where I was a regular kid with good grades and good friends. My parents and I loved living in Boston—we loved walking along the Charles and cheering through baseball games at Fenway. But then two years ago, my great-aunt died and left us her house and store in Samsonville. My dad had just been laid off, so my parents thought a free house and business would solve all their problems. Less than a month later, we moved to the middle of nowhere in Upstate New York.

And the day after we moved, I woke up with magic.

Samsonville was kind of an off-brand Salem—witch trial and all. Hundreds of years ago, four women who worked in Collingsworth's Bakery were charged with witchcraft after the town went hysterical. The magistrate decided the only way to prove the women weren't witches was to drop them in a cage from Holy Cross Bridge into the Keeble River. If they survived, they were witches, and then they'd be burned at the stake. If they drowned, oops, our bad.

Of course, the women weren't really witches. They were all outcasts who weren't liked for some reason, and so they drowned as the town cheered. Years later, some rich guy named John Bryan thought he could make the whole thing a tourist attraction like Salem. He restored the red-brick town square, turned the bakery into a landmark, and even opened a Museum of Witchery. Every year the town did a huge Halloween event and told stories about hauntings, but it was all fake. And nothing was more fake than my great-aunt's store, Occult & Davidson, a spooky gift shop that sold rubber bats, crystal balls, and witch's hats to tourists. All of it completely nonmagical.

I was the only real witch. And no one knew that other than my parents.

But with my powers getting stronger, how long could we keep it a secret?

I pedaled hard toward home, scanning the clouds

like if I kept an eye on the storm, it wouldn't get worse. But that wasn't how my magic worked. It could always get worse.

A raindrop splattered into my eyeball, so I looked down at the steaming asphalt. The roads were empty for the entire mile and a half home. Just pouring rain and me on my yellow bike, as I tried not to scream and cry out of frustration. The more upset I felt, the worse the storm would get, which . . . only made me feel more.

Lightning bloomed overhead, illuminating the sky above me.

Finally, I took a right at the big sign for Occult & Davidson. The dirt-and-gravel parking lot had turned into muddy puddles and streams, but there was only one car there. Old Mr. Day's mint-green Buick was pulling out just as I rested the bike on the side of the gray house. There was a shed in the back, but we never stored anything in there. We'd never been able to get the door to open.

Thunder clapped so loud it made me jump. I ran to the store entrance, glad Mr. Day had already left. Dad manned the shop seven days a week, and Old Mr. Day was usually there six of them. He always had on some kind of hat and wanted to look at the crystals Mom insisted had "special energy," even though he almost never bought any.

"Dad!" I yelled out as bells chimed overhead.

The shop bells sounded higher-pitched whenever I

walked in, like tinkling fairy bells—like the house had given me my own ringtone. My parents said I hit the door a certain way and caused it to change. I don't think they actually believed that, but we went with it.

Dad was behind the register with a book in his hand, but he wasn't really reading. As soon as he saw me, he dropped his glasses and came around the counter. He'd probably suspected the storm wasn't natural.

"Breathe, Em," he said.

He locked the double doors behind us, shut off the lights, and lit eucalyptus- and sage-scented candles—our routine. Then he stood across from me in the softly flickering candlelight.

"I . . . I lost control . . . again," I said.

Admitting that made it hard to breathe. I swallowed against the lump in my throat. My hands shook with power, with the shame of not being able to control my magic or myself. With the helplessness of not being able to get rid of it.

"It happens," Dad said, his voice calm and steady. "It's okay. Just breathe now. In through your nose and out through your mouth."

I wanted to collapse into a ball and cry for the rest of the day. The rain had hidden my tears, but my eyes stung. I was supposed to keep my emotions in what my parents called a "neutral zone" so my powers wouldn't come out, but as much as I tried, it was getting harder and harder. What if the storm had hurt someone this time? What if my powers hurt someone next time? Why couldn't I just be a regular kid again?

"Just breathe," Dad said. "Be here right now. Not in the future or the past. Close your eyes."

Reluctantly, I lowered my eyelids. I tried to focus on the scent of my favorite candles as I inhaled and exhaled, but my heart hammered against my rib cage. The air going in my nose didn't feel like enough. It felt like slowly suffocating. I gasped.

"It's okay," Dad said. "You're okay. Inhale deeper."

He put his hands on my shoulders, and the warmth from his palms felt nice. The store had a way of always being cold even though the house didn't have air-conditioning. I shivered, just noticing that I was freezing.

"You're going to get through this. You can breathe. You'll calm the storm, then change into dry clothes, and I'll make you a cup of tea. You'll be fine. It will all be fine."

I grasped at his words, hoping he was right. I knew he didn't mean any ordinary tea—he'd make me a cup of Aunt Catherine's tea. Right after we moved in, we discovered jars of tea leaves in the kitchen pantry. It was strange, since the house had been empty otherwise, but I'd opened the jars and it was the best smell ever. We didn't know where she'd gotten the tea or where to get more (there wasn't a label or anything), so we saved it for special occasions.

Apparently, lighting up the Keeble counted as a special occasion.

I winced. My magic had done that—struck the river with lightning because of my emotions. What if Avangeline had been hurt? She loved to swim and could've easily been in the river.

And then it hit me: my powers could've killed her.

I started spiraling. My head was light, and even though my eyes were shut, I knew there was lightning outside by the copper taste in my mouth and the tingle in my fingertips. The storm wanted to rage, more of my power begging to come out. It felt like my shirt was the only thing stopping me from splitting wide open. And bursting would've been a relief. Except, what would happen if I completely let go? Part of me wanted to let it happen, but I couldn't risk it. I couldn't risk letting magic hurt the people I loved.

"People have missteps, and they backslide, and that's okay," Dad said. "Losing control doesn't make you a bad person. It just makes you a person who lost control. The important thing is that you learn from it."

He'd said all of this before, and it had worked—I'd stopped a hailstorm in January. But what was there to learn today? The reason I'd lost control was because Avangeline was going to leave. I'd be stuck in this town, friendless and alone. Even worse, I'd never worked up the courage to tell her how I felt about her. Because I didn't know what to say or what any of it meant. I only knew that being near her was like coming back to my own room after a long trip, where everything felt just right. She made the good things in life even better, like a little pinch of salt in chocolate milk. I couldn't pin down exactly when my feelings had shifted, but by New Year's Eve, I'd known that they had. I started thinking of us like the tide and the moon. And the sixteen days she'd dated James had been the worst of my entire life.

Now I'd pretty much lost my chance to tell her. What would be the point, when she had to leave?

"Hey," Dad said. "Hey. You can do this."

I opened my eyes. Rain lashed the store windows, water falling as heavy as a car wash. Thunder roared overhead. The wind howled, and although my dad didn't say it, we both knew the storms were getting stronger. And there was no solution. It wasn't like we could just Google "magic cures." (We had, and the results weren't helpful.) No one knew how to remove or even tame magic, because magic wasn't supposed to exist.

I was not supposed to exist.

And either because I was adopted and/or because nothing had happened until Samsonville, none of us knew how long I'd be like this. My parents hoped it was just a phase, but with each day, I was less and less convinced that this was temporary.

"Whatever is bothering you, we can fix it together," Dad said. "It'll be okay."

I wanted to believe him, but there was no fixing this. Every morning I woke up hoping to be back to normal, which meant that every day I was disappointed by breakfast. I'd wished on every shooting star, 11:11, and lucky penny to be a regular kid again. None of it had worked. The only thing that somewhat helped was meditating, and obviously it wasn't 100 percent, or it wouldn't have been storming outside. And the only thing that would fix Avangeline leaving would be if her parents suddenly fell back in love. And it wasn't like that was going to happen. But—

Oh.

Wait.

What if it did?

Wait, wait, wait. What if they suddenly fell back in love? What if . . . I made them fall in love again?

"That's it, Em," Dad said. "You can do it. Breathe, honey. Call the storm back. That's it."

The rain still fell but not in sheets. The wind stopped blowing as if it would knock down the house. There was a rumble of thunder but not the echoing booms of before.

Because maybe there was a solution to all of this. Maybe having magic would actually help me this time. If I could summon storms and drain color from a towel, neither of which were supposed to be possible, maybe I could make Avangeline's parents love each other again. It made sense.

Kind of.

But I wasn't supposed to use my powers. Mom and Dad had been really, really clear about that. When I was ten, about a week after we'd moved in, I tried to use my powers to clean up the old store. At first it was fine. I'd made a gentle summer breeze to dust everything off, but then I got startled by a mouse skeleton and blew all the merchandise out the front doors, ruining half of it.

My parents had come running outside, horrified by the broken crystal balls and muddy postcards in front of them. We'd spent all weekend trying to rearrange the store and make it nice for the reopening, and I'd just ruined all of our hard work.

Mom had chewed her bottom lip the way she did when there were things she didn't want to say, and Dad had snapped, "Can you please just act *normal,* Emma?"

"Act normal"—that was my parents' motto. Because they wanted a normal daughter who didn't stress them out and cause storms and break hundreds of dollars' worth of merchandise. And instead they were stuck with me. So for the last two years, I'd tried to Just Act Normal.

Dad's theory was that magic was like a muscle, and the more I used it, the stronger it would get, so it was better not to use it at all. But maybe I could harness my powers just this once. Just one time. How bad could that be? The heart was a part of nature, and I could control nature.

Sort of.

I breathed in the scented-candles smell and focused on the warmth radiating from Dad's palms. Water dripped down my calves, and I stood in a small puddle on the plank floor. I'd gone past being freezing, and now I was trembling with excitement. I could do this.

Maybe.

"That's it, Em. Think of a bright, sunny day," he said. "You're doing great. Keep breathing."

Sunshine. Birdsong. The way Avangeline loved to bird-watch, staring at the sky for hours in the spring waiting for bluebirds to come back. How excited she would be, jumping up and down when she spotted one. The perfect way she whistled and how she had the best voice. She should've been a soloist in chorus, but she was too shy to sing alone. The way she had scars on her legs from falling off her bike when she was little and how they peeked out when she wore shorts. She was self-conscious about her legs, but I didn't know why. Her scars were beautiful, like little bits of history tattooed on her skin. I loved how she couldn't help but leave a noseprint on the bakery window when we walked into town. The way she always debated about what to get from Morrisey's ice cream stand, tapping a finger on her chin, but then she would just order vanilla with peanuts and a cherry on top because nothing beat a classic in her mind.

It would be okay. I'd fix everything and she'd stay. We'd have a lifetime together. And maybe one day, I'd work up the courage to tell her how butterflies had filled my chest when our fingers overlapped on a cup of cocoa on New Year's Eve.

"That's it, baby. You've got this," Dad said.

The rain became a drizzle.

I'd figure out how to keep my best friend.

And then the rain stopped.

I looked at Dad. He blew out a long breath, then nodded to me.

"You did it, Em," he said with a relieved smile. "I'm proud of you."

We always left out the part where my powers had caused the storm in the first place, because hey, at least I'd gotten the weather back under control. The winter hailstorm had knocked out electricity to the town for a full day, but I hadn't meant to do that. Really, if anything, it had been James's fault for asking out Avangeline in the first place. He was the most popular kid in school—he could've dated anyone else.

I scanned Dad's face. He'd started getting a few gray hairs in his brown beard and wrinkles by his brown eyes around the time we moved to Samsonville. The vertical worry line between his eyebrows had left an indent, and his white skin was paler than usual. But I guess having a suddenly magical daughter with powers she can't control will do that.

He cupped my face with his hand. "It'll all be okay."

I nodded. I knew what he was really thinking and not saying, because I was thinking it too: what if my powers kept increasing? I'd call hurricanes, earthquakes, and tornadoes, and then what? Climate change could only explain so much. And natural disasters would definitely hurt people, maybe even kill them. And how could I ever be okay with my powers doing that?

We had to hope it wouldn't go that far. That at some point there'd be a limit to my magic. But we hadn't found it yet.

Dad cleared his throat. "Let me go make you that tea."

"That would be great, Dad." I tried to sound bright and happy and, well . . . normal. I'd been trying for the last two years.

"You should go get changed," he said. "You don't want to catch a cold."

He said that because that's what people said to ordinary kids, but we both knew I never got sick. Not since moving to town—not so much as a sniffle, even after both of my parents got the flu bad the first winter. The only time I didn't feel well was when I kept my magic in for too long. We didn't talk about it, but after storms like this one, I felt amazing . . . physically.

"I will. I'm just going to . . . breathe a second," I said.

"Right. Good thinking, Em. I'll be in the kitchen with Aunt C's tea when you're ready."

He walked to the back of the store and through the door that connected Occult & Davidson to our house. I stayed put, a secret plan taking root in my head.

Somehow, I would find a way to keep Avangeline from moving.

3

Once I had on dry clothes, I sat at the kitchen table sipping my tea. The hot liquid warmed me from the inside out and tasted like honey and spices. I stopped shivering, even though my hair was still wet, and I was just . . . calm, almost like nothing had happened. I could even focus on my book and laugh at the funny parts. It was a story about a girl trying to win over her crush while dressed in a hotdog suit. I liked contemporary novels best because, well . . . I had enough fantasy in my real life.

We always had all kinds of books around, because Dad had been a librarian in Boston. He'd loved his job, but he'd gotten laid off because of budget cuts. So my parents had thought it was incredible timing when the next morning they found out that my dad's great-aunt had left us the store and house. I'd only met Aunt Catherine twice, and all I remembered was she was old and unfriendly.

I shivered, thinking about those first days in Samsonville. How strange things had started happening as we unpacked: a moving box sliding across the floor, books floating in the air as I tried to organize them, a lamp cracking when my parents refused to believe that I wasn't just playing pranks on them. After a few days, they saw enough supernatural things to start believing me. And then, just like that, my whole life changed. I went from a normal girl to one with magic.

Suddenly, the kitchen window behind me popped open, letting in a warm breeze.

"I'm okay, thank you," I said. I turned, closed the window, and patted the windowsill.

The house had . . . character. Since we'd moved in, it had seemed to react to me. My parents had thought the house was haunted at first, but then we decided that being around my magic so much must've affected the building, just like how my moods affected nature. I'd gotten used to it. For the most part.

I looked out the window into the sun-drenched garden. Raindrops glistened on the flowers, but none of them looked damaged, which was good, because we cut and sold them as a side hustle. Well, really . . . our main hustle.

My parents had improved Occult & Davidson by

making a website, getting rid of the cheesy rubber bats and fake spiders, and adding local crafts, like the handmade mood ring I'd given Avangeline for her birthday. But they still couldn't lure in many customers outside of fall. Most people only bought pewter skeletons, black cat statues, and crystal balls in October. My parents didn't talk about money in front of me, but the house wasn't all that soundproof. I knew we depended on the flower business. And that business depended on Avangeline.

We had the biggest, best blooms around because of Lina. The first time she ever slept over, it was a warm night and we took a blanket outside to watch the fireflies. When the stars appeared, Avangeline had made me laugh by tracing random constellations like connect-the-dots and then naming them. We'd stayed out so long we'd fallen asleep, and my parents had carried us back inside. The next morning the flowers in the garden were all big and beautiful.

And that happened every time we were in the backyard together. Whether the flowers were in season or not. Whether they'd been in the garden before or not.

At first my parents hadn't liked it. They'd told me to stay inside when Avangeline was over, but Lina had been so wowed by our garden, she'd suggested we bring the flowers to the farmers market. We sold out in the first hour. We needed the money, so my parents allowed me back in the garden, but I knew they didn't like it. They didn't like anything that reminded them I wasn't normal.

Dad built a little greenhouse to try to explain where we could get deep-red roses in the spring and snow-white lilies in the fall. But no one asked why we had such exceptional flowers, except for our neighbor, Mrs. Cornwall. We were surrounded by old farms and woods, so her house was the only one near us for a mile. One day she came over to the garden and stared right at me while saying that it was *amazing* how much better plant life did at our property than hers. Dad had made up some elaborate excuse about soil pH. It had sounded boring and legitimate, and she'd never mentioned it again.

Still, I always felt a little weird around her and couldn't explain why. I got the feeling that she didn't like me, and I didn't like her back. Everyone else thought that was silly. She ran Collingsworth's Bakery—the most popular spot in town. She was literally the most liked and respected person in Samsonville. But I didn't trust her.

I was almost done with my tea when Mom came home. As usual she had her thick brown hair up in a bun, and as usual some strands had escaped. Mom taught preschool in the nearby town of Alder, but in the summer, she was a full-time florist. Today she had been out delivering flowers to the usual homes and businesses.

Mom glanced at the teacup in my hand and frowned, before pretending to smile.

"How are you, my girl?" she asked.

"I'm okay," I said.

She stared at the cup, and I put it down. I'd figured she'd seen the storm, but she might not have if she was delivering to one of the neighboring towns. I should've drunk the tea faster.

"I'm fine, really," I said.

Mom eyed me skeptically while putting a grocery bag on the counter. "Hmm, okay. Emmie, did you have a . . . um, well, was there . . . did you have . . . a good day so far?"

"Mm-hmm." I put the teacup up to my lips.

"Well, I'm just going to talk to your dad, and then what do you say we go into town later?"

"Sounds good, Mom."

She unlatched the heavy wood-and-iron door that connected the house to the shop. The door looked like it belonged in a European castle, not a kitchen in New York.

Mom glanced back at me before shutting the door behind her. Because it wasn't locked, the wood creaked open an inch. The register where Dad sat wasn't that far from the door. (Well, not if you put your ear to the crack to listen.)

I crept up as soon as she left. Unfortunately, my abilities didn't include any super hearing or X-ray vision. Despite all my unruly magic, I had zero superhero traits—I wasn't even tall.

The floorboard creaked under me, the house apparently feeling like I shouldn't listen in.

"Shush," I whispered.

"Hey, Ellen. You made good time," Dad said. Even without being able to see them, I knew he was smiling and tucking the loose strands of Mom's hair behind her ear.

"There was another incident?" Mom asked.

Dad hesitated. "She lost control."

"Oh, Phil. We can't leave tomorrow."

That's right. With everything happening with Avangeline, I'd forgotten that my parents were spending the weekend in Buffalo at a small-business convention. It was supposed to be my first real test of staying home "alone." Not that I'd really *be* alone. One, they constantly tracked me using the Get a Life app on their phones (not the real name, but it should've been). Two, I had to stay with Mrs. Cornwall. I don't think either of us was thrilled with that arrangement, but we'd barely see each other, since she was at the bakery from dawn until dusk. And three, it wasn't for very long—they'd be home before the end of the Founder's Day celebration on Sunday afternoon.

"What if we bring Em with us?" Dad said.

I wrinkled my nose. It was a terrible suggestion. Their trip was business but also the makeup for them not going on their twentieth-anniversary cruise. I had no desire to third-wheel on their lovefest.

Ew. I shuddered. The floorboard groaned in agreement.

"We'd have the same issue with her being alone all day," Mom said. "Phil, what happens if she has another . . . incident and this time neither of us are here? We've been just plain lucky that she's never had one at school."

Dad was silent.

The truth was my parents really needed a vacation. Because of my powers, my family hadn't gone anywhere since moving to Samsonville. The hour drive to Syracuse to see if I still had magic away from town didn't count. (Yes, I did.) And, okay, there was something in it for me too. With them gone and Mrs. Cornwall at work, I'd have the whole weekend to figure out how to make Avangeline's parents fall back in love. To use my powers to fix everything.

I opened the door and walked into the store. I passed the office, where Oliver the cockatoo sat on his perch and Persimmon the cat lazed on the desk. They both gave me curious looks.

"I'll be fine, Mom," I said.

My parents turned and looked at me. Mom worried her bottom lip and shifted her weight from foot to foot. Dad sighed.

"What was it this time?" Mom asked, lowering her voice.

"A storm," I said.

Better to keep it short and sweet. No need to go into how long it raged or explain how lightning had hit the Keeble. No need to make them any more disappointed in me than they already were.

"What happened?" Mom asked.

Okay, I needed to be a little more specific. "A rainstorm."

"I mean what caused it?"

"Just . . . stuff," I said.

Back when we lived in Boston, I used to tell my parents everything. But once my magic showed up, they stopped asking for details, and I stopped volunteering. It was easier to keep secrets than to make them even *more* worried by telling them how the front windows of the house always seemed to sparkle when I got home, like the house was happy to see me. Or that Oliver and Persimmon could talk.

Oh yeah. The cat and the bird could talk. But more on that later.

Anyway, over time it got easier and easier to just keep things to myself. Sometimes I wished they'd ask more, but I understood—they were happier not knowing everything.

"Emmie, I just don't think . . ." Mom trailed off and took a deep breath. "You just had an incident, honey. I don't think this is a smart time for us to go away."

They'd taken to calling the times I lost control of my powers "incidents." I didn't like the term, but it was the safest way to talk about my magic in case someone overheard us.

"You have nothing to worry about, Mom. The incidents never happen close together. I'll be fine with Mrs. Cornwall, and I'll take care of Oliver and Persimmon. I won't get in any trouble."

Mom faintly raised an eyebrow. Okay, maybe I shouldn't have added that last part. No one had mentioned me getting into trouble.

Dad nodded. "She's right, El. The incidents are never close together. The last one was in March."

I smacked my hands on my hips and let my head fall back. "Oh, come on, that counts?"

The wisteria "incident" happened after I'd told a joke with just the right timing. It had made Dad laugh so hard he'd snotted root beer out of his nose. Which had made me laugh until I cried. Which had incidentally made the wisteria on the side of the house bloom in the middle of a late-winter snowstorm.

It wasn't really the same as calling down lightning, though.

"It was noticeable," Mom said.

I pursed my lips. Right. The worst offense.

The number-one rule in our house was that no one could ever know about my "abilities." It was the only secret I'd ever kept from Avangeline. (Well, other than my feelings.) And it was a secret I'd have to keep forever. I'd never be able to let anyone know who I truly was, meaning I'd always have to be a liar. And being a liar was wrong—wasn't it?

But my parents had their reasons.

<u>Reasons No One Can Know You're a Witch:</u>

1. People would freak out
2. People would want to hurt you, take you, or study you
3. People would really, really freak out

I swallowed the lump in my throat that always formed when I thought about hiding and lying for the rest of my life, and then I looked both my parents in the eye.

"There won't be any noticeable incidents while you're gone," I said. "I promise."

Mom and Dad exchanged glances, but I was being honest. I had no intention of anyone noticing anything. If everything went according to plan, no one would ever suspect that I'd used my powers to make Avangeline's parents fall back in love.

— 4 —

Like any supercool twelve-year-old, I spent a lot of time with my mom and dad.

Okay, so maybe it wasn't the *coolest*, but aside from Lina, I hadn't made any friends in Samsonville.

<u>Reasons Emma Doesn't Have Friends:</u>

1. Once I had Avangeline, I never felt like I needed anyone else
2. It turns out keeping a ton of magical secrets creates a barrier between you and everybody else
3. My parents didn't want me to have a bunch of friends

It wasn't that they wanted me to be lonely. My parents were just worried I'd have an incident if I got too excited, so they'd turned down invites when we first moved here until eventually there weren't any. The last party I was invited to was Isabella Miles's pool party in fifth grade. She'd been Lina's best friend before I came to town. I was surprised she'd invited me since we weren't that close, but it was a good surprise because she was also the most popular girl in school. I'd looked forward to it for a month, but then I had an incident right before we were supposed to leave. Mom and Dad wouldn't let me go. I had to call at the last minute and say I was sick. Except someone later told Isabella that they'd seen me at the grocery store with my parents, so she found out I was lying. After that Isabella never really liked me.

Even though I didn't have many friends, because of Lina I never felt uncool or left out. Except when Avangeline went to New Orleans or those two weeks she'd dated James. Then it was the most alone I'd ever felt. If she left for good, I'd always feel that way.

As we took the short drive into town, I silently swore that I'd find a way for her to stay. No matter what.

I stared out the window of our old Honda as we passed over the white stone bridge. Samsonville used to be a lot bigger—a city, not a town. It was full of factories that once employed thousands of people. Now the empty factories stood abandoned on the outskirts and only about six hundred people lived here. Still, there were cool things for a small place, like the old lookout tower by Holy Cross Bridge and Bryan Park, a large green space right along the Keeble. Eight little stores made up the center of Samsonville's downtown. One of them was Collingsworth's Bakery.

"Let's see if we can pick up something for dessert," Mom said as we parked.

I would've been happier just getting Morrisey's ice cream after dinner, but I followed my parents to the bakery.

There was a blue sign on the outside, dedicated to the memory of the women accused of witchcraft. It was now run by our neighbor, Mrs. Cornwall, but she'd kept the original name.

Dad held open the heavy blue door, and I walked into the shop. I always got a weird feeling inside—a chill up my spine that caused me to stand really straight. Maybe it was just the history, but I always held my breath in there and expected something bad to happen. When we'd first moved, I'd asked my parents if they thought anything was strange about the store, and they'd looked at me like I had two heads.

I didn't ask again.

"Hello, neighbors!" Mrs. Cornwall said from behind the counter. When I first met her, I'd thought she was old, but it was just her stark white bob that made her look like a grandma. She was actually around my dad's age. She smiled brightly at us.

"Good afternoon, Mrs. Cornwall," Mom said.

"I guess we should've stopped in this morning," Dad said, admiring the empty shelves and displays. Little chalkboards marked the breads, rolls, muffins, and cakes that had already been sold.

"Oh yes, we were busy all day," Mrs. Cornwall said.

"I see that," Dad said, sounding a little jealous. "Slim pickings."

Even in high season, our store rarely sold out of anything. Collingsworth's, on the other hand, was almost always empty by the end of the day. It had been featured on TV and in magazines and was loved by food bloggers and tourists. They even sold Collingsworth T-shirts. It was such a draw that the mayor had given Mrs. Cornwall a key to the city. (No idea what it was supposed to open.)

The weird thing was I'd never thought the food was good. It wasn't better than anything Mom got premade at the grocery store. Actually, it was worse.

"We were hoping for a dessert," Mom said, scanning the cases like one would suddenly appear. "But I think we're out of luck."

"Well, actually," Mrs. Cornwall said, leaning in like it was a big secret. "I do have a delicious peach pie in the back. I made it for a customer who still hasn't picked up their order, and we're closing soon. It's yours if you want it."

"Really? Sold!" Mom said. Peaches were her favorite fruit.

Mrs. Cornwall smiled, then finally looked down at me. "Anything for you, Emma?"

I shook my head, and she squinted an eye at me, almost like she knew I didn't think her food was good.

"Thank you again for offering to watch her this weekend," Dad said, resting a hand on my shoulder.

I turned and stared. Mrs. Cornwall had *volunteered* to watch me? Why? She didn't like me.

"It's my pleasure," she said.

"You're too kind," Mom said. "Call us if you need anything, Therese, and we'll come right home."

"I'm sure she'll be no problem at all," Mrs. Cornwall said. "Right, Emma?" She glared at me over the counter.

I gulped, then nodded like a bobblehead doll. There was a threat in her voice and eyes, but my parents were smiling like they hadn't noticed.

"Excellent!" Mrs. Cornwall said. "Well, enjoy the pie!"

My mom paid and we walked out. The second we passed through the door, it was like a weight was lifted off my chest and I could slouch again.

"Do you guys . . . You don't think anything is—" I cut myself off. If I mentioned that I found Mrs. Cornwall and the bakery strange again, they might not leave me with her. And then I wouldn't have the time to use my magic on Avangeline's parents. I couldn't risk it.

"What was that, Emmie?" Mom asked.

"Nothing," I said.

And really, how was I going to finish that sentence? Collingsworth's was beloved. Nothing was wrong with it. Even Lina loved it there, humming with joy whenever she got her hands on a mini quiche or pretzel bread, telling me to take a bite because it was so delicious. No one ever got a strange feeling from Mrs. Cornwall except for me.

"Let's put the pie in the car and then take a walk," Dad said.

"That sounds fantastic," Mom said, holding his hand.

When we got to the car, I glanced back at the bakery. Mrs. Cornwall was staring at me through the plate glass window. She smiled when I caught her and waved. I shook it off and waved back. There was nothing wrong with the bakery. It was all just in my head.

5

With buckets of hesitation and 186 reminders, my parents finally left the house Friday morning. The fact that the conference wouldn't refund their deposits probably mattered way more than my promises to be good. Especially since I was supposed to check in *at least* three times a day.

They taped a Closed until Monday sign onto the shop doors and updated their status online, because they didn't think I could run the empty store for three days. Like I couldn't handle talking crystals with Old Mr. Day.

Really, where was the trust?

But after Dad loaded their suitcases in the trunk and they both gave me a million kisses on my forehead, Dad actually started the engine.

I felt a rush of excitement but contained it. The last

thing I needed was to make flowerpots levitate or lights burst while they idled in the driveway.

Once they pulled out of the parking lot and I finished waving at the rearview mirror, I walked up to Mrs. Cornwall's porch and rested my phone on the top step. That way, if they checked, they'd see I was where I was supposed to be. After that I went into our store's office and crashed onto Dad's brown leather desk chair. I needed to get a plan together, and I did my best thinking in there. Plus, I needed help.

"Are they gone?" Oliver squawked.

"Yes," I said.

"I'm surprised they actually went through with the trip," he said. Oliver's real voice sounded more like an old man than a bird.

I shrugged, moving side to side in the swivel chair. "They need the vacation."

"I don't like that you're supposed to stay with Therese Cornwall," Oliver said. "She and Catherine didn't get along."

"I don't like it either, but from what I remember, Aunt Catherine didn't like anyone," I replied.

Now would be a good time to mention that my ninety-two-year-old great-aunt left behind a cockatoo who could fully talk and think like a human being.

He was one of the many mysteries of Samsonville.

It had taken me a while, a long one, but eventually, I got used to Oliver being able to speak. The first time he'd said anything to me, I'd screamed and run out of the room. He later explained that he hadn't started to speak until I moved in. My magic must've changed him, the same way it made the house react to my moods or the flowers in the garden bloom.

"Oh yes, you're oh-so-magical," Persimmon said, rolling her eyes.

Oh. We also had a mind-reading cat.

Persimmon had started talking to me about a week after Oliver did, and it totally freaked me out because cats can't talk—not exactly, not even Persimmon. She couldn't make sounds with her voice box like Oliver. So I had no idea where the voice in my head was coming from. I thought I was losing it, but it turned out Persimmon could read my thoughts and project her own . . . whether I wanted to hear her or not. Which, for the record, was way more annoying.

"I am *not* annoying," she hissed.

I pinched the bridge of my nose. I didn't have time for this same argument again.

I'd never told my parents I argued with our cat. As far as they knew, our pets were normal. They had enough on their hands with me. A mind-reading cat would've sent them over the edge. And I was worried that if my parents knew about Oliver and Persimmon, they'd take them away, to make extra sure that no one ever found out how totally not normal I was. And even though

Persimmon drove me up the wall sometimes, I loved them.

"Listen, I need your help, both of you," I said.

Oliver tilted his head to the side, interested. Persimmon looked at me and then sauntered away. She was a small black cat with huge green eyes and a ton of attitude.

"I'm sorry I called you annoying," I said.

She stopped in the doorway and glanced over her shoulder. "Better, but what's the problem?"

"It's Avangeline," I said. "Her parents want to get divorced. If that happens, she'll move to New Orleans and . . . I'll never see her again. She's my . . . she's my only friend, and she's going to leave for good."

"Oh, Emma," Oliver said, hanging his head. He looked truly sorry for me. Both of them liked Avangeline—even my deeply opinionated and definitely-not-annoying cat.

"You'll always have us." He tapped his foot on my hand.

"Oh yes, and nothing is cooler than a preteen girl with a parrot on her shoulder," Persimmon said, rolling her eyes for the second time in two minutes.

Awful cat.

Oliver ruffled his feathers and squawked at her.

"Did you tell your parents?" Persimmon asked.

I shook my head. "No. Not yet."

The cat quirked an eyebrow. "Why not?"

"Well . . . I'm hoping that while they're gone, I can figure out a way to make Avangeline's parents fall back in love."

Quiet filled the room. I'd done it: stunned my magical animals silent. I turned my chair from side to side, waiting for them to say something, anything.

"That way they'll all stay here," I added, looking from one to the other.

"And how do you plan on accomplishing that?" Oliver asked.

"Well, that's the thing: I don't know." I twisted my friendship bracelet around my finger until I could feel my heartbeat in my fingertip.

Persimmon yawned. "Sounds promising."

"I know, I need to figure it out. I need a plan. And I wanted your help to come up with one, because I was thinking maybe . . ." I lowered my voice to a whisper, even though we were alone. It always felt like someone was listening, although that was probably just my parents making me paranoid. "Maybe I could use my powers."

"No," said Persimmon, the world's worst cat.

I slapped the arm of the chair. "At least think about it."

Persimmon looked to the side for a second. "Okay, thought about it. No."

She stared at me, then nodded, hard.

I rolled my head back and let out a noisy exhale.

Why did I think the grumpy cat would be able or willing to help me? She barely liked me. Of all the unfairness, Mom, the one who was allergic to cats, was her favorite.

"Oliver?" I asked.

He shook his head, the yellow crest on his head waving. "Emma . . . I don't know about this. Human love seems . . . tricky. I observe your parents all the time, and I have yet to understand it. Your mother likes your dad's singing, and it's quite off-key. And your dad says your mom is beautiful, when her hair is very messy. And you know how everyone feels about you using your powers . . ."

I mean, yes, he was right. Just Act Normal was the rule, and my efforts to control my powers weren't . . . predictable. But once wouldn't hurt.

"You're being diplomatic, Oliver . . . or delusional," Persimmon said.

I side-eyed her. To think I was afraid she'd be taken away.

"I don't know, Persimmon," Oliver said. "Maybe she could learn to control her powers, harness them."

"Because using her powers has gone *so* well in the past. Think about what she's done. Poor Carmichael." Persimmon shook her little cat head, her name tag jingling.

My jaw dropped open, outrage flowing through me. "That was mostly your fault!"

I stared daggers at her, but she just shrugged.

Yes, poor Carmichael.

Last summer, I'd won a goldfish in the ring toss game at the county fair, and I'd named him Carmichael. The fish had actually survived the drive home, and we'd gotten him a bowl with a cute little castle. I'd been so excited to win that I hadn't considered how a cat who loved to pounce on anything that moved would react to a goldfish. The answer was: *Oh look, the servants bought me swimming finger food. How novel!*

My parents had put the bowl on the very top kitchen cabinet, out of Persimmon's reach, but nothing is out of the reach of a mind-reading cat.

I came home and caught her with her paw in the water, about to eat the fish. I shooed her away, and after sighing at me, she let him go. But instead of falling back into the bowl, Carmichael hit the rim and dropped off the cabinet. I gasped. I was standing in the doorway, too far away to physically catch him, so I tried to use my powers to stop him before he splattered onto the floor. I kept thinking *air, air, air,* and it worked! He suddenly stopped in midair, a light breeze holding him up.

The joy of success ran through me, but then Persimmon's name tag jingled. I was angry with the cat for trying to eat Carmichael and for being out of the store to begin with, and I lost focus, and, well . . . the fish . . . well . . . he, um, he exploded.

I was inconsolable for days. Mom kept saying that the fish would've died from the fall and he was half-dead from Persimmon anyhow, but even if that was all true, it was not a noble way to go.

That was the last time I'd tried to use my magic on purpose.

I put my head on the desk. I really didn't want to explode Avangeline's mom and dad. But I also couldn't sit back and let all of this happen. Lina sounded like she'd pretty much given up hope, so it was all up to me.

"Guys, I have to do something. Avangeline is . . ." Tears stung my eyes, and I sniffled as I tried to put into words what she meant to me.

Everything. She was just everything.

Oliver walked over and put his head under my hand. I gently petted his soft feathers as I wiped my eyes. Persimmon looked at me with . . . slightly less disdain than usual.

"I have to try," I said, taking a shuddering breath. "If I can calm storms and make flowers bloom, I should be able to help two people love each other again. They loved each other once. How hard could it be to fall for each other a second time? And I need Avangeline . . ." I paused and swallowed hard, but it was like a rock had wedged in my throat. "I need her to stay. And she needs her family whole. You didn't see how upset she was when she told me. I'll do whatever it takes to help her."

"Well, that's understandable," Oliver said.

I looked at Persimmon, and she tilted her head back and forth before giving a small nod.

"How do I do it, though?" I asked.

My animals stared at each other.

Finally, Oliver cleared his throat. "Why don't we start small? Work on controlling your power, any of your powers, first. Let's make sure all the windows are closed, and then you can practice your magic with us."

"Um, excuse me. There will be no animal testing in here, thanks," Persimmon said. The fur on her back stood up, and she hissed.

"I said 'with us,' not 'on us,' Persimmon," Oliver said. "No one is volunteering for that."

I raked my fingers down my face. It wasn't exactly a vote of confidence. But they were right. So long as I was inside the house and the windows were shut, my powers didn't leave the building. Well, except for that one wisteria incident, but we'd figured out that the vines had crept so far into the siding that they could feel my powers even with the windows closed. Dad had trimmed it back, and it never happened again.

But people weren't as easy as flowers. I knew that. Not only would I need to be able to start and stop my powers at will (if I could do that), but I'd also need to fine-tune it to affect only the hearts of her parents (if I could make people fall in love at all). There was also the small fact that I'd never used magic to make anyone feel anything. Never tried to.

I had a lot to learn. And I really wasn't supposed to do this. I paused and thought for a second, doubt filling my head. If Dad was right, trying to use my magic would only make it stronger. Plus, if my parents found out, I'd lose my phone and be grounded for life. I had to hope none of that would happen, but in the end it didn't matter. I'd go through it for Avangeline. Whatever the price was, I'd pay it.

I sat up straight, determined.

"I wish I knew where to start," I said. "I mean, I get not experimenting on anything living, but what should I practice first?"

Both animals thought for a few seconds.

"You could try to light a fire in the fireplace," Oliver offered.

"Or maybe we could try something that isn't the worst idea ever," Persimmon said.

"It's not the worst," he said.

"It is."

Oliver's feathers ruffled as he pointed a wing at her. "Well, what do *you* suggest, then, in all your feline wisdom?"

"She has the most control, if you can call it that, over the natural elements," she said.

"And fire is a natural element," the bird replied.

"Let's not *start* with her burning down the house, Oliver." Persimmon stomped her little foot.

I pursed my lips and looked down at my fingertips.

Unfortunately, she had a point—losing control with fire would be really, really bad. I'd never let flame out because I knew how dangerous it could be, even when anger burned in my chest and it felt like matches striking my arms. Still, Mom and Dad had put fire extinguishers in every room . . . just in case. Avangeline had noticed and said, *"Wow, your parents are really into safety, huh?"* and I let her think that.

"Well, tell us your suggestion," Oliver said.

"Let me think." The cat looked me over from head to toe and then sighed, unimpressed. "Let's do the opposite of fire."

"Which is?" he asked.

"We can have her make ice."

Persimmon loved ice water. Of course there was something in it for her.

But ice did sound like a decent place to start. At least it was better than accidentally torching the house. Even if we put out a blaze quickly, my parents would notice scorch marks and empty extinguishers, and then they'd interrogate me. And since I wasn't even supposed to *be* in the house while they were gone, I'd be in a ton of trouble. Water would be easier to clean up and hide.

"Okay, let's do this," I said. "Should I use the sink in the basement?"

"Let's use a finite amount of water," Oliver said.

"A fin—what does that mean?" I asked.

"A fixed amount," Persimmon said.

I stared at her.

She frowned. "A bowl. I can't even think about what they're not teaching you in school."

I glared at her. "Let me get one, and I'll meet you both down there."

The basement had thick stone walls and no windows, so even if I lost control with my powers, nothing too bad could happen.

I hoped.

— 6 —

I said I was sorry," I said, hurrying after Persimmon.

"Humph!" she said. "I've never been so mistreated in all my life! You're lucky I haven't called PETA and the ASPCA!"

"You can't dial a phone," I muttered.

"Ugh!" She ran up the basement stairs, leaving a trail of water behind her. Because my powers had . . . accidentally soaked her.

I winced.

As I reached the top of the stairs, the steps moaned disapprovingly. "I know, I know," I said, tapping the railing.

"Persimmon, come here," I commanded.

No response.

"Persimmon." I knew she was ignoring me, but I tried anyhow.

I slumped my shoulders as I went into the kitchen and opened the fridge. The cold air hit me, and I shuddered thinking about my attempts to make ice.

It had started well enough, I guess. I'd put a big bowl of finite water on the basement floor, and then I'd taken three steps back. I didn't know why—just seemed like the right thing to do.

Oliver perched on the laundry-folding table, and Persimmon sat near the dryer, both of them a good distance from me. All of us ready for something incredible.

I stared at the bowl. *Ice. Turn into solid ice.* I put my hands out, but nothing happened. Absolutely nothing. The water didn't even jiggle. I pursed my lips and tried harder, but still nothing. Now that I actually wanted my powers, they were no-shows? What the heck?

I flexed my fingers, frustration rising within me. Why could I call in an ice storm but not change a single bowl of water? Magic should follow rules and logic, right? But even the thought was wrong: it was magic, the opposite of logic.

We all stood in the space for so long that Persimmon yawned, lay down, and started snoring.

"What should I do?" I asked, dropping my arms. "I don't get why it's not working."

"Well, let's think about it," Oliver said. "The times your powers have surfaced have all been because you felt something strongly. Your abilities seem tied to emotions—for better or worse. So I don't think concentrating on the water itself will work. For ice, why don't you try thinking about snow and cold things? Try a happy emotion first. Those tend to . . . not go as wrong."

It made as much sense as anything. My happiness had made flowers bloom and sometimes lights burst, but nothing as dangerous as anger, sadness, or disgust.

With my eyes shut, I thought of Christmas. Of presents and getting the decorations out of the boxes. The smell of gingerbread—the only baked good my mom was decent at. I thought about sledding with Avangeline on our favorite hill. Building snow forts just big enough to crawl into together. I thought about her taking me ice-skating for the first time in my life and gripping her hands because I kept sliding all over the place. How the tip of her nose got red like Rudolph in the cold and how she loved frozen ponds. Both of us wondered what happened to fish in the winter, but we could never figure it out. How her favorite drink was hot cocoa made with whole milk and at least seven mini marshmallows. Our hands as they overlapped when I brought her a cup at the New Year's Eve celebration and how I wanted to stay linked like that forever.

I opened my eyes. Nothing had happened to the bowl of water. I stuck my finger in, thinking maybe it had at least turned cold. Nope. Same temperature as when I brought it down. Maybe a couple degrees warmer.

"Think *ice*," Oliver said. "Feel it."

I sighed and tried again. *Ice*. Okay, maybe not winter. Maybe ice on a hot day. Popsicles in the summer, super-chilly air-conditioning, slushies, and Avangeline's tongue stained blue as she drank her favorite: Berry Blast. Brain freeze. Trying to make orange popsicles with juice, which somehow turned out terrible. Eating snow cones with Lina as we watched her brother's T-ball games. And cheering like mad any time he even touched the ball.

Nothing.

"Well, *that* was a resounding success." Persimmon's tail thudded against the dryer like clapping.

Oliver and I side-eyed her.

"All right, let's try to tap into a different emotion," he said. "Ice can be a feeling. How about someone being cold to you? Feeling alone, maybe. Try loneliness."

I thought about my first day at Samsonville Elementary. Looking up and around at the new school building that was much smaller than my elementary school in Boston but way more intimidating since I didn't know a single person. And on top of being the new kid, I was the new kid with secret powers I had to hope I could keep hidden. Otherwise my parents had threatened to homeschool me. Not to mention I was the only Asian person around for miles. I'd brought up the gawking when we drove through town, and my white parents had said people were just looking because I was pretty. Which wasn't the reason, but it was a nice lie, so I let it go.

Other students stared at me, and all I wanted was to be back with my old friends, in my old school, with zero powers.

My new classmates were nice enough, though, and I was lucky that nothing supernatural happened in class, but then it was time for lunch. Everyone had bought lunch at my old school, but I was one of only a few who lined up to buy in Samsonville, and kids stared at me again. I'd gulped hard when I came out with my cafeteria tray, because where was I going to sit? Alone at an empty table, or make people uncomfortable by asking to sit, or . . .

And then there was an arm in the air with a charm bracelet on it. Avangeline used to wear that bracelet all the time—it was her favorite until she lost it in the Keeble. We'd looked for hours and hours but had no luck. Avangeline had been upset about losing it, so I replaced it with a friendship bracelet I made for her. And later she gave me one too. But that first day, there was a smile on her lips and a charm bracelet on her wrist as she waved me over.

"Hey, you're Emma, right?" Avangeline asked.

"Yes," I said.

"Come sit with us." She tipped her head at the space

next to her. Isabella smiled and moved down so I could sit between them. This was pre–birthday party incident, before Isabella decided that she didn't like me.

Later, I'd asked Avangeline why she waved me over, and she just shrugged and said I looked friendly and that it must've been hard to be the new kid in a small town. Her kindness was one of the many things I liked about her.

"You're not focusing at all," Persimmon said.

"It's not easy," I said.

The cat sighed. "How is this hard?"

I sputtered and gestured to the water bowl. "I mean, you try to make ice out of nowhere."

"I'm not the one with powers," she said.

I mean . . . that wasn't exactly true. She was a mind-reading cat.

"The power to manipulate nature." Persimmon's eyes stared at the ceiling before narrowing at me. "You called down a violent thunderstorm because Avangeline was going to leave. So, think about that. What are you going to do if she goes? You'll be alone, won't you? Who will you watch movies with? Who will sit with you at lunch once she's gone? You never bothered to make any other friends."

Every word of Persimmon's was like a dagger to the heart. Pain built behind my eyes and in my chest. I knew all the things she was saying were true. If Avangeline left, my life would be so much worse. Empty. And

Persimmon knew exactly what to say because she was the nosiest mind reader ever.

"You'll be decorating sugar cookies all by yourself at Christmas," she said.

That was the last straw. The sugar cookie decorating contest was Avangeline's dad's thing. Mr. Monroe made a ton of delicious cookies, and his family and friends would all decorate them and then vote on whose was the best. Avangeline had won last December with a cookie that was us in silhouette, like paper cutouts. I'd taken it home and saved it.

"You probably won't even be invited this year, because she won't be there," Persimmon sniped.

I lost it. Anger flooded me. I felt the magic move through my veins, sending the water in the bowl in a wave over to Persimmon. It gathered over her, suspended in the air, and then it fell, soaking the cat.

I wasn't proud.

Persimmon actually had a reason to be mad at me this time—or, well, angry at my powers. I hadn't really done anything. It wasn't like I *told* my magic to soak her. The powers had a mind of their own.

Still, she was only trying to help by getting me to tap into an emotion. But that was the thing. I wasn't ever in control of my emotions, especially not anger, so how could I expect to control my magic?

Maybe this was all a mistake.

I moved a few things around in the fridge and found

the smoked salmon. I thought it was gross, honestly, but my dad and Persimmon really liked it. I guess, looking back, we should've known she'd try to eat Carmichael, since the cat loved seafood.

I took out two pieces of lox and put it on a plate.

"Here, Persimmon. I have a peace offering," I said.

"Humph," she said from . . . somewhere. I looked all around the bright kitchen and didn't see her.

"I really am sorry. I know you were just trying to help."

Okay, soaking her was kind of my fault. Instead of focusing on freezing the water to make ice, my anger had resulted in my tossing it at the cat. Because I'd wanted her to stop talking. That was what happened when I lost focus—my powers just went where my emotions took me. Even that time I caused the windstorm in the store. I'd been trying to help dust the shelves because my parents had been overwhelmed by all the cleaning, but I'd found mice skeletons (thanks to Persimmon's killer tendencies) and got grossed out and lost focus.

I really didn't want to soak or blow up my best friend's parents, so what was I doing?

"Maybe this is a bad idea," I murmured.

"Of course it's a bad idea." Persimmon stopped in the doorway between the shop and the kitchen.

"It's lox." I tilted the plate so she could see it.

She looked to the side like she was debating whether

or not it was worth it to take food from me, even though we both knew I had her favorite treat in my hand. The salt in smoked salmon was bad for cats in big doses, so she rarely got it, but she loved lox. We were lucky she couldn't open the refrigerator, or she'd make herself sick and have to go see Avangeline's mom—Dr. Monroe, the veterinarian.

I bent down and put the plate on the floor so she wouldn't have the indignity of asking. "I can get the hairdryer and dry you off."

Persimmon didn't answer. Instead, she walked up to me and then shook off.

Yes, the cat had waited until she was next to my ankle to shake off her whole body. Water and wisps of black fur pelted me, and I turned my face away before wiping off my legs. I'd have to vacuum the kitchen, because Mom was allergic to cat dander, but I'd deserved that.

Persimmon sat next to the plate and took a few ladylike nibbles before horking it all down. Within seconds the plate was clean. I put it in the dishwasher.

"Well, what do you think we should do now?" I asked.

She stared up at me, totally unamused.

"Obviously no more water, but maybe I could try something else. Maybe I could make seeds grow or potatoes sprout," I said. We had both fruit and potatoes on the counter, and I was good at making flowers grow, so maybe it would be easy.

"I do not feel like becoming the size of a puma, thank you," she said.

I scratched my forehead. I hadn't even considered what would happen if I lost control of my growing power.

"Why don't you ask Avangeline?" Persimmon said.

"She doesn't know about my powers, remember?" I reached into the fridge and got out the iced tea.

It was a small miracle that I'd never had an incident at her house or at school. My parents thought it was luck. My pets thought maybe those buildings protected me somehow, like the house. Or at least put a barrier between me and nature. I thought it was the calming effect Lina had on me. Also, I tried extra hard to stay in control around her because what would she think if she knew about my powers?

It had been hard not to tell Avangeline the truth sometimes, especially when questions like *"What superpower would you have if you could pick any?"* came up. But I also knew that if I told her, she'd never believe me. Or if she did, she'd run away screaming. At the very least, she'd hate me for lying to her all this time. Thinking about losing Lina made it easier to keep the secret. Still, sometimes I felt like Avangeline could never really, truly know me because I would always have to keep things from her.

"I know she doesn't know, Emma," Persimmon said. "I meant ask her what a normal person would do to make two adults fall back in love."

I stared at her. "A normal person?"

"Something that doesn't involve powers, because . . ." She looked me dead in the eyes and shook off again.

Right. It wasn't the worst idea to try regular, Just Act Normal ways to make Avangeline's parents fall back in love. And it had far less of a chance of going wrong.

Probably.

7

Avangeline pedaled up to the house an hour later. Her parents had just started allowing her to bike by herself this past spring, and it always took her forever because she was so cautious. She still wore her helmet and a big smile as she came up the back porch steps. We'd messaged a bunch since leaving the river, and we'd kind of agreed to pretend like things weren't going to change. Otherwise we'd ruin our time together by dreading her move and being sad.

"Hi, Emmie," she said. "It's so cool that your parents let you stay home alone!"

I met her outside with two iced teas and handed one to her. We both liked iced sweet tea with lemon. Mom always had a whole bag of lemon slices in the fridge, since she didn't want me to use a sharp knife.

Lemons: 1. Trust: 0.

"Sort of alone," I said. "I'm supposed to stay with Mrs. Cornwall. My parents think I'm over there."

I stared in the direction of the perfect yellow house where my phone was resting on the porch. Avangeline unclasped her helmet and dangled it from my railing. Then she perched on one of our rocking chairs.

"Which is even better! You get to stay with the world's best baker!"

"I guess." I looked to the side.

"Still don't think she likes you?" she asked.

"I know she doesn't. But I'm just sleeping there, so it doesn't really matter."

We'd agreed to disagree on Mrs. Cornwall a while ago. Lina, like everyone else in town, thought Mrs. Cornwall was great. And I could never explain how I knew that she didn't like me. It was more of a feeling than anything concrete. So I let it go.

"Well, you're *mostly* alone, which is still very cool," Avangeline said. "My parents still think I'm six years old like Max—no matter what I say." She frowned, then bent forward. "Hi, Persimmon."

The snarky little monster was all cute and cuddly as she meowed at Avangeline and circled her ankles. I glared at the worst cat I'd ever known.

"I've only been allowed to watch Max while Dad runs out to get milk or when Mom had a quick emergency at the clinic," Lina added. "And even then I got freaked out and turned on every light in the house. But I'm a chicken." She smiled her lopsided grin before sipping some tea.

"You're not a chicken," I said.

"Oh, I totally am," she said. "Remember when we camped in my backyard?"

Okay, so she was kind of a chicken.

One nice night last September, we decided to go on an overnight camping trip. The only problem was Avangeline and I weren't allowed in the woods by ourselves after dusk. So instead, we camped in her yard. We still got to use our sleeping bags and her orange tent, so it was almost the same, with the darkness and the crickets chirping.

"So, who in our grade do you think is cute?" Avangeline had asked as we lay on our sides talking before bed.

We'd just started sixth grade, and secret crushes were the only thing anyone wanted to talk about. But at that point I'd never had a crush on anyone—not even Avangeline. I'd tried to find boys cute, but I just didn't. My parents said I might or I might never, and either one was fine. Honestly, they were cool about everything . . . except magic.

I'd opened my mouth to answer when there was a strange noise. It was like rattling and snarling at the same time.

"What was that?" Avangeline flipped on the battery-powered lantern and sat up, pulling her purple sleeping bag up to her neck.

"I don't know, probably a raccoon or something," I said, stretching.

Her eyes darted over to me. She looked really worried.

"I'll go check." I unzipped the side of my bag and threw one of my legs out.

"Are you serious?" She reached out and gripped my arm. "What if it's dangerous?"

I shrugged. With my powers, I was always the dangerous one. But it wasn't like I could explain that to Avangeline, so it came off as me seeming much cooler than I was.

"I'll be okay."

"What if it's, like, the Slender Man?" she whispered.

"In your backyard?" I scrunched my nose. "Don't you have to say his name three times or something?"

"That's the Candy—the C-man."

For someone who scared easily, Avangeline also went out of her way to look up scary things.

"Okay, but my money is on it being a raccoon," I said. "I'll take my chances."

"Wait. I'll come."

"You don't have to." I put on my sneakers. "I'll be right back."

"Oh my God, they say that in, like, every horror

movie ever! I'm coming with you!" She flung herself out of her sleeping bag.

"Maybe you should watch less of those," I said.

She pursed her lips but slipped her sandals on.

It was chilly outside, and the early fall night was still. Avangeline had a big, fenced-in backyard because of her dog, Hudson. I took the lantern and started walking around. Avangeline, as promised, came with, but she stayed half a step behind me.

In the darkness I circled the perimeter, trying to see past the fence. The only thing that genuinely scared me was the prospect of stepping in one of Hudson's enormous poop bombs, but we didn't see or hear anything. No Slender or Candy guy or whatever in sight. I tried not to laugh at Avangeline's crouching, nervous walk, because I knew she was really afraid. And I admired how even though she was scared, she wouldn't let me go alone.

I was about to call off the search, but suddenly there was another rattle and snarl. I spun around. Avangeline jumped and yelped, trembling behind me.

It came from the pitch-black shadows on the side of the house.

"Let's get my parents," Avangeline said.

"If you want," I said. "I can go look while you get them."

"No way! Wait for them!"

"Lina . . . it'll be fine." Honestly, whatever it was

had way more to fear from me. Look at what had happened to Carmichael.

"I'm *not* going to lose you." Avangeline took my hand and hauled me up the deck and into the house. She shut the sliding glass door behind me and locked it, her face all resolve.

We found her parents watching Netflix in the living room, sitting on opposite ends of the couch. They stared as Avangeline shook out her hands, trying to calm down. Finally, she got herself together enough to tell them what had happened, and her dad went outside.

Turned out I was wrong: it wasn't a raccoon. A possum had gotten stuck in their compost bin.

So that ended our outdoor camping adventure. Avangeline suggested we sleep in her room that night, and I didn't argue. Normally, we put an air mattress at the foot of her bed, but she insisted I sleep next to her, and she held on to me tight before she fell asleep. I loved going to bed breathing in the smell of her hair, and it was more comfortable in her room than in the tent, so it was a win-win.

"You were brave!" I said. "You investigated the sound with me in the dark."

"Hiding behind you, you mean?" Avangeline put her iced tea on the side table. She smiled slowly. "Like I said: total chicken. You're the brave one."

I laughed, but my smile faded, because how many more nights would we have like that? Maybe a handful before she moved, if we were lucky. But we'd have a lot more sleepovers and adventures ahead of us if I could change things.

"Emmie? Where'd you go?" Avangeline waved her hand in front of my face and then smiled.

"I just . . ." I took a deep breath, then sighed. "I don't want you to go."

She pursed her lips. "I know. I don't want to leave you either. I wish things were different, Emmie. I really do."

We sat in silence as honeybees buzzed around the flowers in my yard. They drifted, wobbling from flower to flower. Avangeline had wanted a beehive to make her own honey after we'd watched a documentary about pollinators last year, but she couldn't have one because Max was allergic to beestings. I'd asked my parents for a hive for my birthday to surprise her. But now if they got me one in July, I'd be beekeeping alone by August.

I groaned inwardly. I really did not want to be a solo beekeeper, any more than I wanted to be the friendless girl with a bird on my shoulder.

"I was thinking . . . ," I said. "What if . . . what if we could make your parents fall back in love? Then you'd all stay here, right?"

She blinked a few times. "I mean, yeah, I think so, since that's the whole problem, but . . . how could we do that?"

This was where controlled powers would've really come in handy.

Persimmon raised a little cat eyebrow at me. Okay. That was a nowhere road. It didn't do me any good to sit around wishing for control.

"Well, I'm not sure yet, but it has to be worth trying, right?" I said.

Avangeline's mood ring was orange—the color of confusion.

"I . . . I don't know, Emmie," Avangeline said, twisting her fingers. "They seem really set on getting a divorce, even though they haven't talked much. Dad's been traveling, so he hasn't been home since Wednesday morning, when they told me and Max. He'll be back tonight, though."

"Is it your dad who wants the divorce?" I asked. From what I'd learned in middle school, there was always someone who wanted to break up first, even if it was "mutual." Mutual just meant the other person was cool with it. No couple had ever said *"This is over"* at the exact same time.

"Well, they said *they're* getting a divorce." Avangeline's face looked stormy, her lips a thin line. "But I think it's mostly my mom."

"Why?"

She shrugged, making one of the straps of her tank top fall off her shoulder. "Mom said marriage is hard and adults just fall out of love sometimes, which I guess sounds mutual, but it was the way she said it. And I overheard my dad say *it* came out of nowhere—it being the divorce, I think. But I know my mom, and she doesn't do anything impulsively, so I just don't understand. And they haven't really explained . . . or listened to me."

Avangeline leaned forward, putting her chin on her hands. I knew what she meant. Lina's mom was nice and everything but . . . opinionated. She always told Lina what to do and talked over her. Lina never could stand up to her, or really to anyone. It wasn't how she was built. But I knew it bothered her.

I pushed her tank top strap back into place. She glanced at my fingers and smiled.

"That's it?" I asked. "That's all they said?"

"Pretty much. Honestly, that's the thing that's been bugging me . . . Well, it all bugs me. But they're not like Isabella's parents, who hate each other. They were fine until they weren't." Avangeline slouched and sipped more tea.

"She didn't say anything else?" I said. "There weren't any other clues that you can think of?"

"Well, not to us . . . but . . ." Avangeline leaned in, and I mirrored her. "I overheard her talking to Aunt Hannah, and she said he doesn't see her anymore. So I think that must be part of it."

Hmm. What did that even mean? Of course you *see* someone you live with.

I stared out into the garden, my eyes landing on the faux greenhouse. My mom had tried to grow some plants in there, and she'd managed to kill them all, even with my powers making everything bloom. Mom had an impressive black thumb—always had. None of our houseplants in Boston had ever made it more than a few days. She even killed a cactus, which . . . you don't water them, so how?

When she tried gardening here, my dad had secretly switched out the dead plants for live lookalikes to make her feel better. It took a while for her to catch on, but eventually she did. I thought she'd be mad, but she just kissed him and said it was sweet to "be seen."

I hadn't known what that meant at the time, but maybe she meant that he saw she wasn't good at something and tried to help. And she liked that. It made her feel special, taken care of. The same way I felt whenever Lina would take the pickle off my plate and put it on hers without me asking.

Then I had an idea.

"Maybe we could help your mom feel seen," I said.

Avangeline tilted her head. "How?"

"Well, we could start by sending your parents flowers from my garden and make them think they're from each other. And do other things like that—setups where it's us but they each think the other is trying to get them back."

I scanned Avangeline's face, waiting for a response. If she'd totally given up hope or if she thought it was a bad idea, she might not say that, but she'd purse her lips.

Her face lit up with a slow grin. "Like, *Parent Trap* them?"

"What's that?"

"Oh my God, okay." She scooted to the edge of her seat. "It's an old movie about these twins who got separated when they were babies because their mom and dad divorced. They were each raised by one of their parents in different countries. They meet at this camp and hate each other, but then they become friends. And they try to make their parents fall back in love so they can all stay together."

"Does it work?" I asked.

"You'll have to watch and see." She stood up and put out her hand for me. "Movie day!"

Okay, this could work. I should've known Avangeline would know the perfect movie for our situation, since she loved films. We could watch *The Parent Trap* and some rom-coms and get ideas on how to make adults fall in love.

I put my hand in hers, and she pulled me to standing.

"Let's have a whole rom-com day," I said. "We can watch and take notes. You still haven't seen *To All the Boys I've Loved Before*."

"Okay. You need to see *The Princess Bride*, anyhow," she said. "It's a classic."

"Oh, and *Shrek Forever After*," I said.

Avangeline wrinkled her nose. "But that's a kid's movie."

"Maybe, but he has to make his wife fall in love with him again," I said.

Plus, I kind of loved that movie. My parents said it was like *It's a Wonderful Life*, but I'd never made it all the way through that one. I didn't tell Avangeline, though—she'd make me watch it.

"Hmm, that's true," Lina said. "Okay, we'll add that one in!"

I glanced down at Persimmon, and even the grumpy cat didn't seem totally against this new plan.

"Okay, I'll run upstairs and get the notebook." I'd gotten a journal with a lock and key when I was ten, and we'd made secret plans in it for the past two years.

Avangeline shook her head. "First snacks, then notes."

We went inside, and I headed straight for the candy cabinet to get her favorite. "Definitely need peanut M&M's."

"And you have to make ramen popcorn," she said.

Ramen popcorn was our invention. My parents always insisted we air-pop our popcorn—something about my dad not liking the chemicals in the microwave kind. The problem was that the microwave kind actually tasted good, and air-popped did not. But one day Avangeline had had leftover ramen seasoning, and I put it on the popcorn because I was too lazy to go get more salt, and it was delicious. And so ramen popcorn was born. Avangeline insisted on it for all our movie watching.

It was something else that I'd lose if she left—the person who not only understood me but also understood the importance of ramen popcorn and peanut M&M's.

I grabbed the jar of kernels. It wasn't going to happen. Not if I had any say in it.

8

So Avangeline was right: I really liked *The Parent Trap*, and that movie was pretty much our plan in a nutshell—well, except for switching places. I hoped her dad didn't have an evil girlfriend already, but I didn't think so, which would make things easier—plus her parents still lived in the same house, so we were way ahead of the game.

After we finished that movie, *Shrek Forever After*, *To All the Boys*, and *The Princess Bride*, we lay on our stomachs on the couch and made the following notes:

<u>E & A's Plan to Get Avangeline's Parents Back Together:</u>

- send them flowers from each other

- send them messages from each other (steal iPads??)
- remind them of the good times
- point out to Avangeline's dad all the good things her mom has done
- recreate how they met (how?)
- put them in a romantic place
- trap them together on a mission (how???)

Some of these were better ideas than others. Some, like trapping them on a mission, were long shots but seemed like they'd work really well.

"There," I said, drawing a flower border around our list.

"When should we start?" Avangeline asked.

"Well, you said your dad is coming home later, right? The sooner the better," I said. "I say we start tonight."

Avangeline pursed her lips. "Emmie . . . I don't know . . ."

"We only have a month to change their minds."

I grabbed her hand, and she smiled. Then she nodded along to a song in her head, the way she did when she was thinking things over. It was one of those little weird features that made her Avangeline. And something I knew I'd miss.

"Okay," she said. "Let me see if you can sleep over."

There were, like, a dozen messages we had to send

to get everyone's permission for me to stay overnight. My parents, her parents, and weirdly, we needed Mrs. Cornwall's permission too, but Avangeline's parents were the hardest to convince. I tried not to be offended, because I knew they liked me. Lina's mother had started sleeping in the guest room, so things had gotten tense, but Avangeline used the guilt card and said that when they left at the end of July, she wouldn't be able to have sleepovers with me anymore. Her mom finally said yes.

I raced up the stairs and grabbed the pink backpack I always brought over to Lina's. It was stocked with a toothbrush, a spare set of clothes, and pajamas. I tossed in another outfit and tore the list out of the journal. I folded the paper, put it in my pocket, and then we were off.

Our houses were about two miles apart—a quick ride . . . Well, it would have been if Lina weren't going super slow. Despite only two cars passing us the entire ride, Lina kept glancing nervously over her shoulder as we pedaled through town, then up her street.

If she moved, the green house wouldn't belong to her anymore. I'd ride by and she would never be home. Nothing would be the same.

I blinked back tears and took a deep breath. I needed to stay neutral, like Mom and Dad always said. Just Act Normal really meant "don't feel anything." Like a robot instead of a person. It didn't matter if I hated it—it mattered that I didn't accidentally call my powers down in front of someone.

We had a plan in place, and I did not need to cause another rainstorm. I focused on pedaling and gripping the handlebars so hard my knuckles turned white, and we made it to her house without a single gray cloud.

The second we opened the door, Max and Hudson came stampeding toward us.

"Lina!!! Catch me!" Max said. He was midair and flinging himself as he shouted it.

"Oof." She swung him down quickly so his head almost touched the ground, and he giggled. "Mad Max!"

Hudson's tail wagged a mile a minute, and I petted him hello. He was the best dog on the planet, and unlike my animals, he couldn't talk (which, given Persimmon, was a good thing). Since he was deaf, Avangeline's mom had made up this cool tapping system for Hudson to feel the vibrations in the floor.

"Emmie!" Max said, looking at me upside down. His brown curls were off his head, spiraling toward the floor. He had big blue eyes like his dad.

"Hey, little man," I said.

He climbed off Avangeline and smiled at me, while keeping a little bit of a distance. I gave him an air fist bump, since Lina was the only one he really hugged.

I loved how she was so great with kids, especially her brother. I liked Max a lot, but since I was an only child, I never really knew what to say or do with young kids.

"Where are Mom and Dad?" Avangeline asked, looking around. It was quiet in the house, aside from the TV in the living room.

"Talking." Max pointed to the sliding glass door that led to the deck.

I exchanged glances with Avangeline. This might be good. Maybe they were talking things out. We couldn't send them flowers or messages when they were both home, but we could show them photos and ask about how they met. Avangeline said they both went to LSU, but she didn't know the details on how they got together.

But maybe we wouldn't need our plan after all. Maybe it had just been a bad fight and an overreaction. Maybe they'd work everything out now that her dad was back. He'd been traveling a lot in the last year, and that was hard on them. Maybe that's why her mom wasn't feeling seen.

I held on to that hope right up until we heard yelling. The three of us turned toward the deck. Dr. Monroe was angrily saying something, but it was hard to tell what.

"You're not listening, Marianne," Avangeline's dad yelled back. It was loud enough for us to hear him through the glass.

Her mom stood opposite him with her hands on her

hips. "Why don't you just keep traveling, then? I'm not sure why you even came back."

"It's my house." Mr. Monroe's dark eyebrows knit, and his forehead creased.

"And you can keep it," she said.

Dr. Monroe came through the sliding glass door and banged it closed behind her. Then she turned and saw the three of us standing in the mudroom.

"Oh." She looked and sounded a little ashamed as she stared at the floor.

"Sure, just walk away like—" Avangeline's dad opened the door and then stopped dead too. "Oh, um, yeah, hey. Hey, guys."

The only noise in the house was the cartoon on the TV, and Hudson huffing and wagging his tail because he couldn't hear them fighting. I'd never seen them fight before, and I'd gone over there at least once a week for two years. I didn't understand how things had fallen apart so quickly.

I didn't know what to say, and I guess no one else did either.

"I'm just . . ." Mr. Monroe began. Then he cleared his throat. "We were . . . There was a . . . Well, I was just about to go to the store."

Avangeline's mom glanced at him out of the corner of her eye. "You do that."

"Yeah," he said. "Anyone need anything?"

"Marshmallows!" Max said.

Their dad smiled. "That's not really needing something, buddy. We'll see."

He skirted around us, ran his hand over Max's curls, and then left. The garage door opener hummed and an engine started, and then he was gone. We all looked from the door to Dr. Monroe.

She side-eyed the garage and pressed her lips together. "Well, I need to make a call. Make yourself at home, Emma. Max, honey, go clean up the LEGOs. I'll fix dinner soon."

With that, she left too.

Avangeline's face fell. Her mood ring turned cobalt blue for sadness.

"Let's play LEGOs." Max grabbed her hand and pulled her forward. Max loved LEGOs, even though he never wanted to take his creations apart.

Lina shook off her expression and gave Max a small smile. "Sure . . . while we clean up, like Mom said."

I watched them walk down the hall together. As I stood all alone, I realized this was going to be much harder than I'd thought.

9

Avangeline sang a clean-up song with Max while I fed some greens to Coffeecake, their rabbit. He was cool, even if he didn't like to be picked up. He did, however, love being fed, so he climbed into my lap while I gave him some bok choy.

Hudson abandoned us as soon as Dr. Monroe started making dinner. We were having filet mignon with mac 'n' cheese, which was one of my favorites. The mac 'n' cheese was from a box, but (don't tell my dad) I liked that kind better.

When dinner was ready, I helped Avangeline set the table. Lina's family always had formal dinners, with a tablecloth and fancy glasses and stuff. Dr. M. handed everyone plates with steak and mac 'n' cheese. Avangeline looked at hers. She was a vegetarian, but her mom always forgot. She eyed her mom but didn't say anything. Still, everything was fine . . . until Mr. Monroe came home with a bag of marshmallows.

I guess he hadn't really needed to go to the store, since that was the only thing in his hands. The four of us were eating—me, Avangeline, Max, and Dr. Monroe. As Mr. Monroe paused in the doorway, I noticed there wasn't a place set for him. Dr. M. had given us the plates—just four of them.

"Um, hey, Dad," Avangeline said.

"Guess I missed dinner," he said, looking around.

"Well, who knew how long you'd be at the *store*," Dr. Monroe said.

"I understand. Wouldn't want a box of gourmet mac 'n' cheese to go to waste," Mr. Monroe said.

The room was silent as my eyes bulged out of my head. I didn't know where to look, so I stared down at my plate. Out of the corner of my eye, I caught Dr. Monroe glaring at Avangeline's dad.

"You can have my steak," Lina said.

"And half of my mac 'n' cheese," I said. I'd already finished my steak. I was saving the mac 'n' cheese in case Lina was still hungry.

"It's okay, girls. I'll just have a soda."

"But I don't eat—" Lina began, but I could barely hear her because she was muttering to the tablecloth.

"You do that," her mom said. "Ava, honey, eat your steak."

"But she—" I said. Lina shook her head at me. She didn't like to rock the boat with her mom. She cut into her steak, but I knew she wouldn't eat it.

Her dad went into the kitchen, grabbed a drink, then sat at the head of the table. He normally sat at one end, with Dr. Monroe at the other. My parents always sat next to each other.

I looked at Avangeline, wondering if we should start our plan in order to break the tension in the room. She shook her head a little, but she couldn't have known what I was thinking—it wasn't like she could read minds. I pulled the list out of my pocket and looked at it under the table.

Point out to Avangeline's dad all the good things her mom has done.

Right. Easy enough.

"This dinner is great, Dr. M.," I said.

"Thank you, Emma," she said.

"It's yummy," Max said. He shoved another heaping spoonful of mac 'n' cheese in his mouth.

"I bet it is," Mr. Monroe said. He took a long sip of his soda.

I winced.

Dr. Monroe dropped her steak knife. It clanged onto her plate. She cleared her throat and opened her mouth, but then she looked at me, Avangeline, and Max. She picked up her glass and drank some water, even though I swore she mumbled something.

Okay, so that hadn't worked out. But on our list there was also recreating how they met, which we couldn't do because we weren't sure how they'd gotten to know each other. But I could ask. Maybe it would end the fight and they'd remember a better time. My dad always did a cheesy redo of his first date with my mom on their anniversary, complete with a terrible Boston accent and red-checkered tablecloth.

"So, um, my parents are at a seminar in Buffalo this weekend," I said. "My dad actually went to college out there—at UB. Where did you guys go to school?"

"I went to Tulane," Dr. Monroe said.

"Like your dad, I went to state school—Texas A&M," Mr. Monroe said. "We couldn't all go to fancy private schools."

I glanced at Avangeline. I thought she said they met in college.

Dr. Monroe laughed. "Yes, I lived at home to save on room and board, and I had merit scholarships for my fancy school. But then again, I didn't have a daddy paying for me to party every night in a frat house."

Mr. Monroe's face flushed.

So this was worse. I needed to get them back on track.

"But wait, how did you meet if you went to school in New Orleans and you were in . . . Texas somewhere?" I had no idea where A&M was. Did the A stand for Austin?

I waited for Avangeline to chime in, but she was staring at her water glass like it was super interesting.

"Oh, we met when I was at LSU—that's where I went to veterinary school," Dr. Monroe said.

Mr. Monroe nodded. "I was looking at LSU for my masters, and they were playing A&M, so I went to Baton Rouge for the football game, and Marianne was there. We both got stuck in a long line for the concession stand."

"I didn't know that," Avangeline said, blinking.

"Mm-hmm, they had, like, one register open for a full stadium," Dr. Monroe said. There was a little bit of a smile on her face. "We were standing there for so long, we started talking to each other."

Her dad smiled too.

Joy raced through me, and I carefully exhaled so I wouldn't make anything weird happen with my powers. But this was working! I dug my nails into my palm to counter the happiness, but I could see the glow on their faces. They were remembering the good times.

"What your mom doesn't know is I'd seen her passing by—we almost knocked into each other as I came out of the restrooms," Mr. Monroe said. "There she was, this beautiful girl in a purple LSU shirt. She didn't give me a second glance, but I couldn't stop staring at her. I lost her in the crowd a minute later, though—there were almost a hundred thousand people at that game. When I saw her at the concession stand, I jumped in line behind her. I wasn't going to miss my second chance to meet her."

Avangeline and I stared from one to the other. Mr. Monroe looked directly at Avangeline's mom, and she gazed back at him.

"But you never . . ." Dr. Monroe began.

I gripped my chair seat. This could be it. Their moment. Like in *Shrek Forever After* when they had that spark while fighting. Okay, yes, I'd watched that movie too many times, but still. I waited, holding my breath, for something magical to happen.

"I'm done," Max said. "TV?"

Dr. Monroe shook her head slightly, like she was waking up from a trance. Then she looked at Max. "Sure, buddy."

With every kind of distraction possible, including knocking over a water glass, dropping a fork, and banging into the buffet, Max left the room.

"What did you talk about in line?" I asked, hoping to pull them back into the moment.

"Oh, honey, I don't know. That was a long time ago." Dr. Monroe stood and gathered her plate and utensils. "I need to go to the clinic and check on some cases. You're fine to watch the kids, right?"

Avangeline's dad nodded, but his eyes tracked her leaving the room.

"We talked about a snack mutiny and what kind of

treats we'd make if we took over the stand," Mr. Monroe said. He was answering me but looking at Dr. Monroe. "I hit her up with an 'Excuse me, miss, could you tell my family I went down fighting?' And she turned around like I'd lost my mind, but it got her talking to me. I said something that made her laugh and I was hooked. It was all I wanted to do—hear that laugh again. I took her out after the game. Then the next day and the day after that. And then I moved to Baton Rouge for this girl I'd known for a weekend. And it was the best decision I ever made."

Avangeline and I both stared at her mom. Lina looked hopeful, her chin rising.

Come on. Say something nice back.

I stared at her mom's back, trying to will the words to come out.

Say it. Stop right there. Turn around and move your lips. Open your mouth.

Suddenly, Dr. Monroe stopped short in the doorway and turned around. Her mouth opened, but no words came out.

My eyes went wide. Whoa. Wait. Wait a second. Had I done that? Had my powers made her stop and then forced her mouth to move?

No, that wasn't possible.

Lina's mom shook her head like she was confused. "Um, like I said, girls, it was a while ago."

Then she turned around and left.

It was all I could do not to groan as Mr. Monroe's chin dropped a little. He balled up a napkin and then released his fist.

"Well, who wants dessert?" he asked. "I could make you some s'mores with the marshmallows."

"I'd love one," I said.

"Sounds good, Dad," Avangeline said. She didn't like s'mores, but she was probably trying to cheer him up.

"Great," her dad said. "I'll ask Max if—"

"I want three!" Max yelled from the living room.

Avangeline's dad smiled, but his eyes were still sad. I wanted to tell him that everything would be okay, that we'd figure it out. That I might've been able to make Dr. Monroe stop and move her mouth just by willing it. But I could never tell anyone that, and adults didn't like when kids tried to help with grown-up stuff anyhow.

So I didn't say anything, and he left the dining room.

Still, the night had been a success. We'd learned how they met, and more importantly, we now knew it was Dr. Monroe who we had to get to fall back in love. It was clear Avangeline's dad still loved her mom. That was a huge head start—we just needed one person to change their mind instead of two! And the biggest success was that I might've been able to use my powers, and actually control them, without anyone realizing it.

Maybe.

I was so excited that all I wanted to do was spill to

Avangeline. I turned and faced her, but then I remembered I couldn't tell her. No matter how much I trusted her, there were always things I couldn't say. I'd have to wait and tell Persimmon and Oliver later. I deflated a little but smiled.

"Well . . ." I said.

"That was a disaster," Lina whispered.

"I don't think it went badly," I said. "Next time we can—"

"No, Emmie." She shook her head. "We made it worse. I know them. All we did was upset them."

"We can fix it." I reached out and grabbed her hand.

She squeezed mine back. "We can't."

"Sure we can, if we—"

She frowned. "No, Emmie. No." She said it hard and final in a way I rarely heard from her lips.

I sat there, stunned. "But I don't understand."

She sighed. "I liked the idea that we could make them fall back in love, so I went along with your plan, but interfering won't work. We have to accept that they're going to get a divorce."

"But, Lina . . ."

I couldn't believe she was saying this. We'd barely even tried—how could we quit now? Especially when things were looking up?

"I don't want to upset my mom any more," she said, the worry line appearing on her forehead. "She has to have her reasons—she always does. It's just done."

It was hard to remember to breathe, because if we didn't interfere, they'd get a divorce and she'd leave and then everything would be awful. And I'd just been filled with so much hope because I might've actually focused and controlled my magic. This whole night was like a bad roller coaster. I splayed my hands on my legs, rubbing the nubs of my kneecaps to keep calm.

"But the way he looked at her and the way she looked at him . . ." I began.

"I mean it," she said. "No more."

Before I could get another word out, Avangeline reached over and tapped her friendship bracelet to mine. I gasped, eyes wide. A friendship bracelet tap meant it was final—no more arguing. I needed to promise we wouldn't intervene anymore. Immediately.

We'd created the bracelet tap as an unbreakable promise after seeing Annabelle and Pacey's friendship go up in flames in elementary school. They'd been as close as we were, but an argument about something small had snowballed, and now they hated each other. Real nemesis stuff. Avangeline had been asked to choose sides, and she'd picked no one, so they both didn't talk to her anymore. After all that drama at the end of fifth grade, we'd come up with the tap. It meant whoever pressed it first got their way, and the other person had to accept it. It was an agreement to put our friendship first, before anything else—even being right. We rarely used the tap, but it was important.

"Okay, Avangeline," I said, staring at my bracelet. Lina had woven the pink, blue, and green threads together for me. Hers was yellow, blue, and purple. "I swear we won't interfere anymore."

She nodded and rested her hand on my shoulder. "Thank you, Emmie. I know this isn't what we planned, but this is the way it has to be."

Lina stood and grabbed her plate. I took mine and followed her into the kitchen. Her dad was on the patio getting a fire started for s'mores, and she began to load the dishwasher.

I sat on a stool at the kitchen island and watched her. The dimple on her cheek showed, the way it always did when she was really focused on something. A few curls fell into her face. She brushed them aside, then caught me staring at her and smiled.

We exchanged glances, and as usual so much swelled inside me that I wanted to say, but nothing came out. For a split second, she seemed disappointed, like she wanted me to finally tell her everything, but then she smiled again. And I knew in my heart I couldn't let her go.

I'd meant my friendship bracelet promise, though. I'd never break that. *We* wouldn't interfere with her parents anymore. But that didn't mean *I* wouldn't. She just couldn't know.

10

It's hard keeping new secrets from your best friend when you already have a bunch of old ones. So I left Avangeline's house right after I got dressed on Saturday morning. She was a late riser, so she was still asleep at eleven when I hopped on my bike.

I pedaled slowly, thinking about ways to make Avangeline's parents fall back in love. I couldn't send them flowers anymore, because Lina would know I'd done it and broken my promise. And I couldn't steal their iPads or anything like that without her help.

What could I do on my own? A tiny voice in my head said maybe I shouldn't do anything, but I couldn't leave it alone. I just couldn't. I could take Oliver to the vet to talk to Dr. Monroe. Maybe claim he hadn't been feeling well (he'd object to it, but whatever). That way I'd get some time alone with Dr. M., and I could remind her about the good times they'd had as a family.

But that might not work. Talking about how they met had only affected Avangeline's dad, not her mom. And she'd probably tell Avangeline that I brought Oliver in. Lina was too smart and knew me too well to believe that my bird just happened to be sick.

So that was a no.

Pointing out the good things Dr. M. did hadn't worked, and I couldn't recreate how they met, because it wasn't like I had a stadium with a concession stand handy . . .

But wait, Founder's Day was tomorrow.

Every year the whole town, like, all 610 of us, got together for a big picnic to celebrate the founding of Samsonville. There was grilled food and music. What if I had a bake sale? I could sell cookies and cake. Maybe get enough people interested that there would be a long line and then Dr. M. and Mr. Monroe could be stuck in the line again and . . . yes, it was perfect.

I leaned forward, putting all my weight on the pedals because I had to get home. I had some baking to do!

Except . . . wait: I didn't know how to bake.

I squeezed my brakes and came to a stop on the shoulder of Holy Cross Bridge. It wouldn't be hard to Google how to bake desserts, but my mom didn't want me using the oven because she was worried I'd burn the house down. Not to mention that I was supposed to be at Mrs. Cornwall's. But how was I going to make cookies or cakes without baking?

I gripped my handlebars, standing with the bike between my feet.

Shoot. It was the perfect plan. Now what?

I looked back at the town, and right across the river was Collingsworth's Bakery. All right, I couldn't cook, but I could buy a cake and sell some slices. Mom did that sometimes when she needed to donate for bake sales. Collingsworth's was closed on Sundays, so maybe Mrs. Cornwall wouldn't mind the competition. I could even advertise her business and donate the proceeds to charity.

Yes, a charity bake sale. That would work!

And I would need the donation, since I only had eight dollars on me and that wasn't enough to buy a cake.

I rode back across the bridge and jumped off my bike in front of the blue-and-white storefront.

Bells chimed overhead as I entered the bakery. It was late Saturday morning, so it was the busiest place in town. There were five people ahead of me in line, more coming down the sidewalk, and the three little tables in the back were all full.

Mrs. Cornwall was smiling and ringing people up. She never had a hair out of place—even now, as she was calling out orders to her staff and numbers for people waiting.

It always smelled so good in the bakery. Today it was the scent of rosemary rolls, fruit pies, and little savory quiches. The food just didn't taste as good as it smelled. At least to me.

An out-of-towner walked by moaning into a cupcake.

Only to me.

Mrs. Antonio smiled at me as she left with her French baguette. She was around my grandma's age, with long white hair. Her husband had passed away last year. He was a nice old man who'd been the other regular in our store aside from Old Mr. Day. Mom had donated free flowers for the funeral and had made me go to "pay our respects."

I didn't know the other people in line, but I did recognize their accents: New York City and Boston. People came all the way from Europe to try Mrs. Cornwall's food. She'd even been offered a cooking show, but she'd turned it down to man the shop. Honestly, sometimes I thought something was wrong with my taste buds.

Bells chimed again, and Miss Sophia came in. She was the town librarian and super nice. I'd overheard my dad telling my mom that Miss Sophia's fiancé had died years ago in a skiing accident, and she'd never gotten married after that. My parents were both friends with her. She bought flowers from them almost every week, and Dad loved to talk about library stuff with her.

"Hi, Miss Sophia," I said.

"Oh, hi, Emma. How are you?" she asked.

How was I? Scheming, lying, desperate . . ."I'm good."

"Read anything great lately?" She smiled, and even though she was an adult, she actually wanted to know. Miss Sophia kind of reminded me of Belle from *Beauty and the Beast*—if Belle were around my mom's age. She wore long dresses and always had a book in her hand. Even her brown hair was kind of the same.

"I just finished *Hot Dog Girl* and loved it," I said.

"Oh, that's a good one! It's not witchy, though."

When my powers first surfaced, my parents and I had researched where they might've come from. I'd asked Miss Sophia for help and recommendations. She'd pointed out witch books to me ever since. Awkward, but she just thought it was a normal interest from a normal girl whose family ran a place called Occult & Davidson.

"I think I'm done with my witchy stage," I said.

"Hmm, I'll select some different reads, then, for you if you want," she said.

"Sure, that would be great."

I moved close to the counter, since I was next.

Mrs. Cornwall stared at me like she was surprised to see me. "Hello, Emma. Did you have fun at your sleepover?"

There was something odd about the way she asked the question—her tone, I think. But I let it go. "Yes. Thanks."

"So what's all this about witches?" She wiped her hands on her white apron.

"Oh, we were just talking about books," I said. "Some novels."

"Hmm, well, I can always tell you about the history of this bakery if you want. What can I get you?" Mrs. Cornwall said. "I made some lovely quiches if you haven't had breakfast yet."

I hadn't eaten, but I was too amped up to worry about my stomach. "Oh, I already ate. Actually, I came here because I was hoping you might want to donate a cake for a bake sale tomorrow."

Her eyebrows were dark even though her hair was white. She raised one at me. "A bake sale? On Founder's Day?"

"I thought it would be a good opportunity to raise some money," I said. "Since everyone will be at Bryan Park."

"Money for what?" she asked.

Shoot. I totally had *not* thought of a cause. This was why I needed Lina. She was always better at thinking things through.

"Well, um . . ." I looked around. Miss Sophia looked at me like she was waiting for the answer too. Right. The library—that could be a cause. They could always use more money for new collections. "I'd rather not say right now."

I tipped my head toward Miss Sophia.

"Oh. Okay," Mrs. Cornwall said. She paused and thought for a second. "I'm sure I can whip something up. But you can also have whatever's left in the shop at the end of the day."

I rocked on the balls of my feet—this was working out way better than expected. "Wow, that would be great! Thanks, Mrs. Cornwall."

Mrs. Cornwall smiled, and I went from happy to hesitant. An icy feeling spread across my chest. Why? Why did I always get this bad feeling from her? Maybe I was just looking for trouble. She was fine. We'd lived next door to her for two years, and she'd never done anything to us. In fact, she'd volunteered to watch me.

"After church, of course," she said.

"Church?" I asked.

"Tomorrow is Sunday." She said it like it couldn't mean anything other than church.

My parents had never been religious. They'd raised me to be nice to people, say please and thank you, and not talk with my mouth full. But Avangeline's family went to the same church as Mrs. Cornwall. Sometimes I went with them. It was boring but okay.

"Right. Of course. Church." I took a step to leave.

"I'll see you at home later, then," she said. "I assume you're not sleeping at Avangeline's again."

"I'll be home."

"Yes, you will."

I smiled, but I didn't miss her strange tone.

I was still looking back at her when I went out the door. A second later, I bumped right into someone.

"Oh, sorry, I—"

"You should look where you're going, Emma," Mrs. Miles, Isabella's mom, said.

"Oh, leave her alone—it was an honest mistake," Mr. Miles said. Isabella's parents were *always* fighting.

Mrs. Miles sputtered. "She almost knocked Isabella over!"

"You're exaggerating, as usual," Mr. Miles said.

"Oh, so now this is *my* fault?" Mrs. Miles shouted.

"I'm okay, Mom," Isabella said. She gave me an apologetic smile.

Of course I'd bowled into Isabella and she'd been nice about it. She had thick dark hair, bangs, and two dimples I was always a little jealous of. I guess I was always a little jealous of her in general, if I was honest. It was hard to believe that Avangeline was best friends with me when she could have stayed best friends with Isabella.

"Sorry," I said.

"It's really no big deal," she said, cool as ever. "Why don't you guys go ahead?" she said to her parents. "You don't want someone to take your spot in line."

More people were coming down the sidewalk, and her parents hustled inside.

"Sorry about them," she said, sighing. "As usual."

"It's okay," I said.

We stood in silence for a second. It always seemed

like she wanted me to say something, but I never knew what. After she'd caught me lying, I never apologized because it wasn't like I could tell her the truth, so I'd left the lie alone. It seemed wrong to apologize for getting caught lying and then tell another lie to get out of it. But sometimes I wished I hadn't messed up the chance for us to be friends.

"Will you be at the Founder's Day thing tomorrow?" she finally asked.

"Um, yeah."

"Cool. Maybe I'll see you and Avangeline there," she said.

I smiled as she went inside. It was weird that she hadn't mentioned Avangeline moving, but maybe Lina hadn't told other people yet. Maybe she was still secretly hoping that her parents would change their minds.

Maybe it could all work out.

Hope filled me like a hot air balloon. I got on my bike and rode back to my house, whistling in the off-key tone I'd inherited from my dad, trying to stay in my neutral zone and ignore that the flower baskets in town bloomed as I passed by.

— 11 —

Once I got home, I checked in with my parents and dropped my phone at Mrs. Cornwall's. Then I ran up my porch stairs. They creaked cheerfully under my feet, like they were happy to see me.

I dropped my overnight bag on the porch and unlocked the doors to Occult & Davidson. I looked around, but neither animal had come out to greet me. Typical. Persimmon refused to meet me at the door "like some kind of dog," and Oliver was usually reading.

"Persimmon! Oliver!" I called. "I'm home."

"Emma?" Oliver said in a birdlike voice from inside the office.

I strode through the store, past shirts that said "Bewitched by Samsonville," and stopped in the office doorway. Oliver was standing on the desk, reading yesterday's newspaper. (Today's hadn't come yet.) I always left it out for him. My parents figured it was for a litter box, but really, he liked to read current events.

"I have something to tell you . . . Wait, where's Persimmon?" I asked.

Oliver sighed. "On a hunt."

I sighed too. Persimmon was a killer. Not just goldfish; all small creatures were in danger when she was in the mood for murder. We fed her well, but that didn't matter to the little serial kitten, because nutrition wasn't the point. So we tried to keep her locked inside, but somehow she always found a way out. I suspected Oliver helped her unlock or open doors, but we'd never caught him and he'd never admitted it.

"Come on," I said. "Let's go find her."

Oliver flew onto my shoulder, and I went back outside. It was a nice Saturday, but heat prickled my skin as we walked around the porch to the back garden.

The small black cat was in the middle of the lawn, lying on her belly batting a chipmunk around—playing with her food. Aka: torturing a poor living thing.

"You stop it right now!" I said.

The loudest huff filled my brain.

"Oh good. You're home," she said.

I folded my arms across my chest. "Let it go, Persimmon."

She stared at me, and I stared back. I was going to win this contest. No murder on my watch.

She sighed. "Be free."

She released its tail, and the chipmunk was so scared it ran right into her chin. She looked at me and opened her mouth, all sharp teeth ready for carnage.

I stared daggers at her. "Don't you dare."

"You're not exactly a vegetarian, you know," she said. "How do you think steak winds up on a plate? The cow just gives it to you?"

I pursed my lips—Lina had made a similar point. But Persimmon didn't kill the chipmunk. The poor animal wobbled away.

"I need to eat. You don't need to kill. We feed you," I said.

"Tomato, to-mah-to," she said. "They kill the things in my food too. What's the difference?"

"I . . ." I didn't really have an answer for that.

Persimmon sent a particularly smug "humph" into my brain.

Oliver looked back and forth between us.

"What did you want to tell us, Emma?" he said.

Ugh, I'd gotten off track arguing with Persimmon. Again.

"So I was at Avangeline's house last night—" I began.

"We know," Persimmon said.

Great. She was going to be salty all day about me ruining her crime spree.

"I know you know," I said. "My point is last night I think I . . . I think I controlled my abilities." Joy spread through my body, and I took a deep breath to make it go away.

My animals stared at each other.

"What do you mean?" Oliver asked.

I dropped my voice to a whisper. Persimmon could hear me no matter what, and Oliver had great hearing. "I wanted Lina's mom to stay in the room and to move her lips, and then it happened. She stopped in the doorway, and her mouth moved."

I waited, expecting them to be astonished, but both animals were silent for a while.

"Is . . . there more?" Oliver asked.

"Well, no." I fiddled with the hem of my shorts. Why weren't they as excited as I was? Actually, they didn't seem stoked at all.

"And it's not just a coincidence because . . . why? Oh, right. It is a coincidence." Persimmon flopped down on her side, tired of me.

"I don't think it was," I said.

"Because you don't want it to be," she said without looking up.

"But I really felt it. I wanted her to stop and move her lips, and she did. No words came out, but I know *I* did it."

The bird and cat were weirdly silent.

I took a deep breath. "Anyhow, I think I can really do this tomorrow. I'm going to have a bake sale to recreate how Avangeline's parents met. They should already feel at least some kind of old happiness being in line again, and then I'll make them fall back in love."

Silence again.

"So, to recap," Persimmon began.

Oh, here we go. I tipped my head back and waited.

"You believe you can fine-tune powers you've never been able to control and make two adult human beings fall permanently back in love *tomorrow* because you might've been able to make one person stop in a doorway for a second, but you couldn't actually get her to speak?"

"Well, I—"

"Love it. No notes. Flawless plan. Let me know how it works out for you." Persimmon stared at me and then pounced on a fly.

She did not, in fact, think it was a flawless plan.

"Oliver?" I asked. He'd flown off my shoulder and was perched on the railing.

"I . . . Emma . . ." He paused and preened his feathers. "If you really focused your abilities, that is a huge accomplishment and you should be very proud, but it may be too big of a leap to go from making someone stop walking to making them fall in love. With time I'm sure you could do it, but tomorrow . . . So much could go wrong around so many people."

I bit the fleshy inside of my lip. This was not going the way I'd hoped. I wasn't sure if they even believed me. But even if they did, they didn't think it mattered. And that stung. They didn't think I was enough.

"Stop being dramatic," Persimmon said. She rolled an acorn in front of her. "Here, if you're in control all of a sudden, prove it. Make a tree grow, and we'll believe you."

"I—" I hesitated, suddenly not feeling very confident. All my magical failures came rushing back into my mind.

But Persimmon was right—I needed to make sure I had full control now, or tomorrow would be a disaster. But how had I controlled my magic? It wasn't an emotion bursting out of me like most of the times my powers had shown up—I'd just wanted it really badly. In my head, I'd told Avangeline's mom to stop and open her mouth, and she'd done it.

Maybe I could do it again.

I stood at the top of the back porch stairs and focused on the acorn. Really focused on the little stem, ridged top, and smooth base. We'd learned in science class how a tree sprouted. So now I just had to make that happen.

But Persimmon distracted me by dashing up the steps.

"That was a close call," she said from behind me.

"Hey!" I said at the same time Oliver said, "Yes, it was."

"Maybe we'd be safer inside the house," Persimmon said.

The bird agreed, and they slipped inside the kitchen door and then sat on the windowsill.

Safety: 1. Trust: still 0.

But I needed to ignore them and focus. It didn't matter what they thought so long as I could actually make a tree grow—that would *show* them.

With the sun beating down on me, I walked up close to the acorn.

I wanted to see a tree. A pretty one, blooming in the center of the yard. Avangeline and I could sit beneath it and eat fresh fruit.

Break the shell. I want a tree right here.

I focused on the acorn but more on wanting a tree. Green leaves and how they rustled in the wind. The rough feel of bark under my fingers. The strong limbs that supported me when I climbed. The birds that made a branch their home, and how I could see the nests when the trees were bare.

No one really believed in me, but that was okay: *I* believed in me. I could do this.

The acorn moved.

I gasped. I was really doing this!

Joy raced through me, and instead of trying to make it go away, or trying to stay neutral, I put all the feeling into one command: *Grow.*

Suddenly, a green shoot appeared out of the acorn—a plumule, we learned that in science class. I didn't know if Persimmon and Oliver could see it from the window. Probably not, since the acorn was in the grass. Still, I'd done that. It wasn't a coincidence or the wind. I wanted to turn and look at my animals, but I was afraid if I broke my focus, it would stop . . . or go haywire.

Grow.

Next, the radicle came out.

I lifted my hands a little at my sides. *Now grow.*

The first leaves sprouted. The stem thickened and it was an actual sapling. I started in surprise, and the sapling bent into a U shape. I refocused and the sapling straightened, getting larger and taller until it became a young tree almost up to my waist. Even from the kitchen window, I was sure anyone could see that I was growing a tree, a real tree, in the middle of my yard.

Pride swelled in my chest, and the tree suddenly doubled in thickness—no good. I exhaled, calming down, and reached my arms higher. The tree narrowed back to normal and grew to nearly my height. I splayed my fingers, and more branches appeared. As flowers grew on the branches, I realized that I was growing a peach tree—not a tree that grew from an acorn. A peach. My mom's favorite.

Victory flowed through me. I'd done it! I had control . . . mostly. Last night wasn't a fluke or coincidence. My powers were responding to me.

I focused on growing the tree past my height. Using my magic made me feel warm and happy with myself for the first time in a while. All I thought about was the tree until a voice said, "Well, isn't that unusual?"

I spun around, and there was Mrs. Cornwall, standing near the shed with her arms folded.

"Hello, Emma," she said.

I stared at her until there was a loud *thud* behind me. I jumped and looked back. The new tree had fallen, dead and gnarled, onto the center of my lawn.

12

"I . . . I can explain," I said.

My heart beat into my throat as Mrs. Cornwall calmly raised an eyebrow at me.

"I would love to hear it," she said.

Okay, I couldn't really explain. I breathed hard, trying to contain my emotions, but what did it matter? She'd already seen my magic. I dropped my chin to my chest and silently studied the ground. She took a step closer.

"You don't have a reasonable explanation because there isn't one," she said.

A cold feeling ran across my back, and I shivered in the heat. It didn't seem like lying would help at this point.

"I knew something strange was going on here," she said. "Come with me."

Reluctantly, I followed Mrs. Cornwall away from the dead tree. As I walked, the reality of what I'd done started to hit me: I'd shown my powers to someone else. Undeniably. Once my parents got home, I'd have to tell them that I was practicing my magic (which I shouldn't have been doing) right outside where anyone could see me (which I *definitely* shouldn't have been doing). I'd be grounded for weeks, and they probably wouldn't go out of town again until I was thirty.

And why in the world had I thought that using my powers outside was a good idea? Because Persimmon had goaded me into it? Mom and Dad weren't going to believe that our magical cat had double-dared me. And I'd also get in trouble for not telling them that we had a magical cat. They'd probably take Persimmon and Oliver away, and then I'd have no one.

I pinched the bridge of my nose. I was in it deep no matter what. My palms sweated, and I really wished I had the superhero ability to disappear or fly away.

I turned to look back at Persimmon and Oliver, but Mrs. Cornwall started speaking again.

"Haven't you learned this town's history?" she asked, her voice cold.

"Yes, ma'am, I have."

I shuffled my feet, kicking pebbles in my driveway

as we continued marching toward her house. What was I going to do now that our next-door neighbor, who really didn't like me, knew my biggest secret? It wasn't like I could erase her memory. She'd probably call my parents as soon as we got inside. And what would my parents do? We would probably have to change our names and move before anyone else could find out. And then what about Avangeline? What would happen to us?

A whirl of wind started inside me.

No. I couldn't let that out. Maybe there was a solution to all this. Maybe my parents could buy Mrs. Cornwall's silence? But what did that even mean? I'd heard it on a TV show once, but never in real life.

Panic spun in my chest as question after bad question filled my head. I tried to tamp it down. To not feel the chaos inside me so it wouldn't become a tornado. But I was losing the battle. And could tornadoes really pick up houses and move them somewhere else like in *The Wizard of Oz*? That might work.

We walked up the stairs of Mrs. Cornwall's porch, and she stopped and faced me. I grabbed my phone, clutching it so hard I thought I might break it. My heart hammered in my chest, and I tried to focus on being calm, but I was breathing way too fast, and my head felt light and dizzy. I wanted to puke and disintegrate all at once.

Mrs. Cornwall looked down at me.

"Don't you know what they do to people like us?" she said.

Every thought suddenly left my head as I blinked at her. I even stopped hyperventilating. Had I just heard her right?

"People like . . . us?" I said.

"Witches." She stared at me. "Open casa."

With a wave of her hand, her front door swung open, and she gestured for me to go inside.

13

The inside of Mrs. Cornwall's house was spotless. There was a dining room to the right, a sunny living room to the left, and a dark wood grandfather clock in the hall. Every room looked like it should've been on those home shows my mom watched. And the place belonged to . . . a witch.

Mrs. Cornwall pointed to the left, and I went into the living room. A couch and two chairs flanked a fireplace. And just like my house, it was chilly inside. Goose bumps coated my arms.

"Have a seat, Emma," she said. "I'll make us some tea."

Mrs. Cornwall went out through the swinging door to the kitchen, and I perched awkwardly on the floral-patterned couch cushion. I was both cold and sweating.

I jostled my legs, anxiously waiting for her to come back.

My neighbor was . . . a witch? That was impossible. I was the only one with real powers. But I'd seen with my own eyes how her door had opened when she commanded it.

So there were other witches.

Wow. It felt like my brain had shattered.

But what if Mrs. Cornwall knew where my magic came from and how it worked? My stomach flipped, but this time with excitement instead of dread. Maybe I could find out why I was like this. I rubbed my palms on my legs in anticipation and to warm up my hands.

A few minutes later, Mrs. Cornwall reappeared with a brass tray and set it down on the coffee table. There were two fancy teacups, a teapot, and some shortbread cookies. I was a sucker for shortbread, but I was too excited to eat.

"Are you cold, dear?" she asked, looking at my legs bobbing up and down.

Before I could answer, she spun her fingers toward the fireplace and said, "Alight a flame." Instantly, fire lit up the logs.

I stared at the roaring fire as she poured the tea. It was real. There was warmth coming off it.

"Are you really a witch?" I blurted out.

Mrs. Cornwall smiled as she sat down in the chair across from me. Then she lifted her hand and said,

"Aloft, plate to the air." The plate of cookies levitated until she dropped her hand. "Settle to the tray."

The plate gently floated down, back to where it had been.

"Yes," she said. "I'm a witch." But she was out of breath like she'd just run a mile in gym.

"Is something wrong?" I asked.

"It's just the toll of casting."

I tilted my head. "Toll?"

"The aftereffects of using magic," Mrs. Cornwall said.

Huh. I'd never felt anything but good from using magic.

I finally understood how my parents must've felt when I made furniture move or flowers sprout. Because even knowing there was magic, even being a witch, I couldn't believe there was another one in the room with me. With precise control like I'd never dreamed of. My mind kept trying to find a logical explanation: an optical illusion, the tray floating on magnets or thin string, or something. But no, it was magic. And magic really freaked people out.

"How?" I asked. *How* and *why* were the questions I'd wondered the most for the last two years.

She sipped her tea and then set it gently in the saucer. "How, what?"

"How do we have powers?" I asked, my mouth dry.

Mrs. Cornwall tilted her head. "How are we witches?"

I nodded. She said it like it was just a normal

conversation. Like she wasn't astonished to be in the room with another witch. How was she being so calm?

She squinted at me. "You really don't know, do you?"

I shook my head. "I've never known where my powers came from or why they happened. I'd been normal until I came here, and then I woke up and had these . . . abilities."

"Interesting." She sat up even straighter. "That must've been very frightening for you—to think you were the only one with all this power."

I nodded.

"It must have been very lonely too. To not have anyone understand your abilities."

I gulped as tears pricked my eyes. That was it: loneliness. The thing I'd been feeling since I first woke up in Samsonville. My parents never wanted to talk to me about magic, and I always had to hide it from Avangeline. But Mrs. Cornwall understood.

"Well, Emma, there's magic everywhere, just like there's air—invisible to the eye but powerful and necessary. And there are places in the world, like Samsonville, where the magic is more concentrated. No one knows exactly why magic pools in certain areas, but it's similar to how there are places with more water than others. And there have always been those who are attuned to magic, who can use it, and those who cannot."

I leaned forward. "There are more people like you and me?"

She frowned. "There were. Witches were once common. For as long as there have been people, there have been witches."

"But what happened? If magic is still all around us, why aren't we common anymore?" I asked.

She pursed her lips. "As the world evolved, it got . . . busier. Noisier. And people lost touch with magic. Magic is difficult to wield and takes time to learn, while technology is easy and doesn't have a toll to it. Some skills vanish and die when they're not needed anymore."

"So it was just that the world became more modern?"

"Well, that and jealousy. There have always been those who couldn't manipulate magic but wanted to. And as the connection between people and magic became rarer, those who were still able to use it were seen as different. Dangerous. So they were hunted down. Sometimes privately and other times by a whole town."

Mrs. Cornwall gestured with her hand. Here. She meant here.

"The Samsonville witch hunts were . . . hunting actual witches?"

She nodded. "But practicing magic was a dying art even back then."

"So the women who worked in the bakery . . ."

"Were witches," Mrs. Cornwall said. "They were distantly related to me on my mother's side. The bakery has always been in my family."

"Wow," I said.

I sat back and stared straight ahead. There was so much to take in. So many answers were overloading my brain that I just stayed quiet.

"They were foolish and got caught," Mrs. Cornwall said with a pointed look at me.

Heat rose into my cheeks, and not from the fire. The comment hung in the air as Mrs. Cornwall nibbled on a cookie. But one thing she'd said stood out.

"So magic runs in families, then?" I asked. "The ability to use it, I mean."

"Yes and no. Spells are honed generation to generation, but only my great-grandmother practiced magic—no one else in my immediate family had the ability. Witches typically pass down their knowledge to the next relative who has an affinity."

I blew out a breath. Man, my life would've been so much easier if I'd had a relative to show me how to use my magic. To let me know I wasn't alone these past two years. I'd been born in Korea. Were there people there who could've helped me? And if so, what happened to them? Why had they given me up? It had never really bothered me, this birth family on the other side of the globe, but now I wished I could at least know if they were witches.

"However," Mrs. Cornwall continued, "sometimes no one in a witch's family will be able to wield magic, and then a witch's knowledge dies with them, unless they can find an apprentice—someone born with the affinity but no witch to guide them."

Everything in me perked up. Me. She was describing me—a person with an affinity for magic but no one to guide them.

"An apprentice?" I asked slowly, trying out the word on my tongue.

Mrs. Cornwall leaned forward. "You and I are the last of a dying kind, Emma. I don't have any children, and I haven't sensed affinity in my nieces or nephews. You could be my apprentice."

Hope filled my chest, and I pinched my thigh because I was never supposed to feel anything too deeply—otherwise lights burst, flowers bloomed, *noticeable* things happened. But was there really someone like me? Who could teach me? And was she somehow sitting right in front of me? It was more than I'd ever thought possible.

"You'd show me how to use my powers? I mean . . . how to use magic? To control it?" I asked, talking fast. I tripped over the phrasing. This whole time I'd thought the power was coming from inside me, when I was just using the magic around me.

Mrs. Cornwall nodded. "I've practiced since I was around your age. While witches are born with affinity, they come into their powers at different times, and of course, some never do. But they always need each other. That's why there used to be covens—to share knowledge, to protect each other, and also to hone abilities. As I said, practicing magic takes time and patience, trial and error, like learning any skill. But a rogue witch isn't in anyone's interest."

No, I knew for a fact it wasn't.

My mind flooded with wonder. A coven. That's what we could have.

I'd been wrong about Mrs. Cornwall this whole time. I'd found something off with her energy, but it was because she was also a witch, not because she was bad or anything. That sinking feeling in my gut must've been me sensing her affinity for magic. I stared at her with new eyes, finally seeing her for who she really was. I smiled, and she smiled back. And then I thought about her smiling at me in the shop.

"So the bakery is . . ." I began.

"Enchanted, of course." She shrugged. "Magic makes people believe that my food is the best thing they've ever tasted."

"But . . . why?" I asked.

She raised an eyebrow. "I would've thought that with your parents' shop floundering, you'd understand a bit more about business. It's about money, Emma. I don't ever have to worry about paying a bill or attracting customers. My magic is only temporary, though." She paused and frowned. "And it doesn't work on you."

"Why not?"

"Because you need consent to enchant another witch." She took a sip of her tea as the pieces came together for me. *That's* why I didn't feel the same way about Collingsworth's as everyone else. It wasn't in my head—the food really wasn't anything special . . . except for the magic.

But as much as I knew businesses struggled in town, it seemed kind of wrong for her to enchant everyone. Would I enchant people if it helped my parents? I wasn't sure.

But I was trying to enchant Avangeline's parents. So maybe it wasn't that bad.

"So tell me, what spell did you use? And where did you find it?" Mrs. Cornwall said.

I knit my eyebrows. "Spell?"

"Yes, what words did you say to grow that tree?" She placed her teacup down. Mine was still sitting there untouched. "Peach trees don't just grow out of acorns," she added with a grin.

"I . . . I didn't use a spell."

Mrs. Cornwall turned her cup handle. "Emma . . . I know you've had to keep your identity a secret all this time, but you don't need to lie to me."

I shook my head. "I'm not lying."

She narrowed an eye at me. "You didn't say any words from a book? You're telling me the tree just grew like that in front of you?"

I stared down at my hands. "I . . . it's been like this since I moved here. Things just . . . happen with my powers. With magic."

"Without any conjure words?" she asked.

I raised my palms and shrugged.

She lifted her chin, looking down her nose at me. "So the tree just grew for no reason?"

"I wanted it to?" My voice rose at the end like it was a question. I hated when I did that. I cleared my throat and resolved to speak with more determination. "I wanted it to."

Mrs. Cornwall's face changed. There was a certain look in her eye, but I blinked and it was gone.

"I see," she said. "What other things 'just happen'?"

I drew a deep breath. "Storms, winds, earth moving, flowers blooming, a firefly swarm once, lights bursting—that kind of thing. And I don't want them to, but they just . . . happen when I feel things strongly. It's only lately that I've been able to get my powers to do what I want them to."

"Lately as in . . ."

"As in . . . last night and today."

I grimaced. It really didn't sound impressive.

Mrs. Cornwall was silent as she stared at me. She studied me for so long that I fidgeted under her gaze.

"But you could help me control my magic, right?" I asked.

She smiled. "Of course, my dear. You are a very powerful witch, and I am experienced. Together, anything is possible."

I let that wash over me—*anything*. Even making Avangeline stay.

14

The phone rang and I jumped. Everything Mrs. Cornwall had said about witch hunts made me feel like villagers might come and take us away at any moment. Mrs. Cornwall eyed me.

"Excuse me for a minute, dear." She went into the kitchen.

I sat thinking about everything she'd said, everything I'd learned. It all made sense . . . in a magical sort of way.

The kitchen door swung open again.

"I'm sorry about that. My staff had questions about the shop," Mrs. Cornwall said, sitting down.

"It's okay," I said.

My phone dinged, and I took it out of my pocket. "Sorry, my parents will freak if I don't answer them right away."

"Of course," Mrs. Cornwall said.

But it wasn't my parents. It was Avangeline asking if I wanted to meet in the woods in thirty minutes. Of course I did. I wanted to spend all my time with her. Only, how much would we have?

"Something wrong?" Mrs. Cornwall asked.

I looked up from my phone, and she was staring at me.

"No, it's just Avangeline. I'm going to meet her soon."

"I see," she said.

There was that look again. Like she'd picked the lock and read my journal and knew all my secrets.

"I hear Avangeline is going to be moving away," Mrs. Cornwall said.

"What?" I asked loudly. I shifted and accidentally hit my knees into the table, spilling tea from my cup. "Where did you hear that? About Avangeline?"

"Dr. Monroe mentioned that she was going to miss my red velvet cake, so I connected the dots," Mrs. Cornwall said casually. "It's soon, right?"

"End of next month," I said. "I hope she stays, though. I've been trying . . ."

I trailed off, remembering I wasn't supposed to tell anyone about my plans. Not even Avangeline.

Mrs. Cornwall raised an eyebrow. "You've been trying to what?"

I spun my friendship bracelet on my wrist. Yes, I was supposed to keep secrets, and I still didn't entirely trust her, but Mrs. Cornwall had already discovered I was a witch. We were way past hiding things.

"I've been trying to figure out a way to make her parents fall back in love. She's only going to move because her parents want to get divorced, and . . . I can't let that happen."

Mrs. Cornwall laced her fingers on her lap. "Some people would say that if her parents have fallen out of love, it would be wrong to change their free will."

I sighed, my shoulders slumping. It was the kind of thing I expected an adult to say.

"I know," I said. "I know I should leave it alone. And Lina said to let it go, but . . . I can't."

"You'd use magic to change their minds?" Mrs. Cornwall asked. This time she raised both eyebrows.

"I would, but I don't . . ." I sighed, twisting my fingers. "I don't know how. I've been trying to control my powers, but . . ."

But there was a dead peach tree in my yard.

"Yes, love is a tricky thing," she said.

"I tried nonmagical ways. That's why I wanted to have a bake sale—to recreate how they met . . . kinda. I was hoping that if I put them in a similar situation, they'll feel something again. Because . . . I don't know anything about love."

I crumpled, putting my elbows on my knees. I was hoping I could make her parents fall in love, but the truth was I had no idea how to do it. I didn't even know how to tell Avangeline about my own feelings. I was worried she didn't feel the same and worried I'd mess up the friendship permanently by spilling my guts and then I'd have no friends even if she stayed.

"No, I suppose you don't," Mrs. Cornwall said with a frown. "But I may be able to help."

I snapped my gaze to her.

She smiled, lifted two fingers, and turned her wrist. "Appear, book of mine."

All of a sudden, out of thin air, an old leather-bound book landed in Mrs. Cornwall's hand. My mouth fell open. I rubbed my eyes, but there was nothing wrong with my vision. A book really had appeared out of nowhere.

"Is that . . . a spell book?" I asked.

It was mesmerizing. I couldn't take my eyes off the worn brown leather or the stones embedded in it. Magic shimmered on the book. I could feel it both pulling me in and pushing me away.

Mrs. Cornwall ran her hand over the cover, and the crystals glowed. "Every witch from a family of witches has one. It's how our knowledge is passed down through generations. But spell books must be kept hidden."

"Why?"

"Well, because of villagers, of course."

"Oh."

"But just like how every family has recipes, every family has different spells. The more knowledge a witch has, the stronger they can become. So that knowledge must be protected at all costs."

It made sense. If magic was a skill like anything else, the more you knew, the stronger you'd be. Dad said reading was like that. He always told me that knowledge was power.

"But, of course, you and I can share our knowledge," Mrs. Cornwall said with a grin. "If we stick together."

Excitement made my pulse quicken, and I sat at the very edge of my seat. Knowledge was exactly what I needed. "Is there a spell in there that will make people fall in love?"

"Let's see, shall we?" She looked at the book. "Turn to love."

With a flick of her wrist, the book's pages moved until it was in the middle of the foot-thick book. The pages were old—maybe parchment or vellum. Okay, I'd never seen either in person, but it definitely wasn't printer paper.

Her eyes moved along the page, and then she stopped.

"Away to the ether." She waved her hand up, and the book vanished.

I stared at the air where the book disappeared. How was that possible? How did something vanish into thin air? I guess it made as much sense as making flowers and gusts of wind appear out of nowhere. Still, I blinked one eye at a time and looked again from different angles like maybe it was an illusion. Mrs. Cornwall sat quietly.

"Did you see anything that would help?" I asked.

"Just the thing, actually: a love potion."

I scratched my forehead. A potion? "Something they'll have to . . . drink? There aren't words to say?"

She shook her head. "Remember, Emma, it's too dangerous to openly practice magic. Potions keep the spells hidden."

Right. Okay. There was a lot for me to learn. But that made sense. Except, wait . . . potions were real? Like in *Shrek 2*?

"Does it work like I think?" I asked. "I get them to drink the potion, then they'll instantly fall back in love?" I couldn't hide how eager I was, rubbing my hands together like an excited little raccoon. "I slip it in their coffee or something?"

"Well, they can't know they're drinking a potion, of course," Mrs. Cornwall said. "A long time ago, villagers used to pay witches for potions and tonics, but we're long past that." She paused and glowered. "And it's hard to slip it into a drink without them knowing, because there's always a . . . taste to them."

"Oh." I sat back a little. How was I going to get them to drink something that had a strong taste without them realizing it?

"Of course, there are always ways to hide it," she said.

"Like what? How?" If I sat forward another inch, I would've fallen off the couch.

"In flavored food. Sugar naturally dulls the senses.

And you need a cake for your bake sale tomorrow, correct?"

"Yes."

She stroked her chin. "I can bake the potion into a red velvet cake—Dr. Monroe's favorite. Yes, that would work. Cream cheese frosting already has a strong flavor."

A love cake. It was exactly what I needed! But I hesitated . . . it was almost too good to be true.

"You'd do that for me?" I asked, wide-eyed.

"Of course, Emma. You and I together can do anything . . . If we help each other, our power will be unstoppable."

"That would be amazing! Wow. Thank you, Mrs. Cornwall!"

Joy lit up through me, and I couldn't hold it in. I felt the blast of giddiness flow along my limbs, shooting out of me before I could contain it. I stared at her lamps, bracing myself for them to crack, but . . . nothing happened.

I blinked a couple of times, confused. At home that feeling would've shattered light bulbs. Once, Mom and Dad had made a dinner so delicious that my powers had broken the light above the kitchen table. Glass rained down, ruining the food. And that joy wasn't a tenth of what I'd just felt. My powers must've really been changing quickly.

Mrs. Cornwall stood. "You go play with your friend while I rest. I'll need to gather the ingredients for the potion at midnight."

"Wait, why midnight?"

"Because that's the witching hour—when magic is at its strongest."

"Oh."

There was so much for me to learn. But now I had someone who could actually teach me!

We walked over to the front door, and Mrs. Cornwall opened it with her hand. A blast of heat hit me from outside.

"One more thing, Emma," she said. "You need to swear you'll keep what we discussed today a secret."

"I . . . of course," I said.

"Say you consent—you agree not to tell anyone."

I knit my eyebrows, but she kept staring at me, so I nodded. "I swear not to tell anyone."

She swirled her fingers. What felt like a ribbon wrapped around me, but I looked and there was nothing.

I stared at her. "What was that?"

"It's a binding promise between witches to keep us both safe, dear," she said. "Until I release you, you will not be able to share what you heard in here about me or magic—as we agreed."

Oh.

"Go and have a good time, Emma," she said.

With that, she ushered me out of the house, and I stood on her porch, wondering how on earth I could keep all this a secret.

15

I walked back to my house, even though I still wasn't sure how I could keep what I'd learned from a mind-reading cat. Then again, I'd sworn not to tell anyone, and animals weren't *anyone*—they weren't people—so, technically, I could tell them and still keep my promise, right?

My dad sometimes called me Little Miss Loophole, which I didn't like, but I was starting to get why he said it.

I opened the kitchen door. Persimmon and Oliver were waiting for me. That was a surprise.

"Emma, what happened?" Oliver asked.

"We were so worried," Persimmon said.

I stared down at the little cat, closing the door behind me. "You were?"

"Well . . . Oliver was worried," she said. "You know how he is."

I raised an eyebrow at her. "I heard *we*."

"No."

"Eh, it was a pretty distinct *we*."

She rolled her eyes. "You want me to like you, but you also want to talk. Choose one."

"Enough," Oliver said. "What happened? What did Therese Cornwall say?"

I opened my mouth, eager to answer, but my mind went blank. I blinked a few times, trying to remember. What had happened? I knew Mrs. Cornwall had caught me practicing magic, and I knew we went to her house. We talked and then . . . and then . . . I couldn't remember a single word that was said. It was like a movie with the sound off. I could picture us sitting there having tea and cookies, but every detail of our conversation was gone. And I should've been worried, because it was like I'd blacked out, but for some reason I wasn't bothered by it.

"We talked . . . Everything was . . . all right," I said.

"Are you okay?" Oliver asked.

I patted myself. Physically, I was fine, so I nodded.

"Your mind is empty," Persimmon said.

I shot the cat a dirty look. "Hilarious."

"No, I mean I can't read . . . anything about what happened over there. Your thoughts are blank. Something happened to you." The cat looked me over, her green eyes even bigger than normal.

"I'm okay, really. Mrs. Cornwall must not have caught me. We had a really calm conversation, and that wouldn't have happened if she'd seen me making a tree grow."

The kitchen was silent as my animals looked at each other. Then my phone chimed.

It was Avangeline. That's right. She'd messaged asking if I wanted to go to the woods, but I'd forgotten to answer. I texted back that I would meet her at our usual spot by the Keeble.

"I'm going to go hang out with Avangeline, but let me give you guys fresh water and food," I said.

I emptied and refilled their bowls and started digging around the refrigerator.

Oliver flew up in the air so he was at eye level with me. "Emma, wait, I don't like this. We saw the tree, and it was incredible, but did something happen to you over there? Why can't you tell us about it?"

I shook my head, even though it felt like I was missing something. But it couldn't have been that important if I'd forgotten.

Oliver opened his beak to speak again, but then there was singing. It was coming from outside. I looked out the window, and Avangeline was riding up to the house on her bike. I shooed the animals back inside the store.

"We'll talk later, I promise," I whispered.

They both started to object, but I shoved the food at them, then closed the heavy wood door and locked it.

With a big smile, I opened the kitchen door to the porch. But the second I stepped outside, I remembered: Mrs. Cornwall was a witch.

My smile fell and I stumbled back a step as the memory of our conversation came flooding in. My neighbor was a witch from a family of witches. She *had* caught me making the tree grow and then told me all about how magic worked. She had a spell book and was going to make a potion cake. And I'd sworn I wouldn't tell anyone. And she'd . . . bound me.

That was why my mind had gone blank—so Persimmon couldn't read it. So I would *have* to keep my promise.

An icky feeling crept across my chest. I'd have to keep this secret no matter what.

I tried to tell Lina as she pedaled up the driveway. I tried to shout, "Mrs. Cornwall is a witch!" But nothing. My tongue wouldn't move. No loopholes.

I knew that Mrs. Cornwall wouldn't have done anything wrong to me—she was the most loved person in town. But something about the way she'd bound me seemed . . . off.

I didn't have time to think about it, though, with Avangeline right in front of me.

"Lina," I said. "What are you doing here?"

As usual, she still had her bike helmet on as she climbed the stairs.

"Oh, you know, I was just in the neighborhood . . ." She smiled her lopsided grin. "You didn't answer my text earlier, and I got worried." She paused and wrinkled her nose. "I definitely sound like my mom right now."

"I'm sorry. Actually, I texted you back a few minutes ago," I said.

"Oh, I must not have felt it," Avangeline said. "But I'm the one who's sorry." She clasped her hands in front of her and looked down.

"What? Why are you sorry?"

"For the bracelet tap last night. Is that why you left this morning?" She stared at me, her eyebrows raised in the center.

"No. No, I just needed to get home to take care of Oliver and Persimmon. And I . . . I decided to have a bake sale tomorrow. So I needed to get everything together for that."

Avangeline tilted her head. "Really?"

"To raise money for the library," I said.

She knit her eyebrows. "You didn't mention it last night."

"There was a lot going on, and I only figured out how to do it today. But Miss Sophia works so hard and the teen section could definitely use new books. I figure with the whole town together for Founder's Day, it'll be a good time to get donations, and then I'll surprise her with all the money."

I wasn't lying to Lina—that really was the plan. I just wasn't telling her the whole truth.

"That's really cool. What should I do to help?" Avangeline asked.

"I think I have everything."

"Oh . . . okay." She looked deflated, her shoulders slumping. Then I remembered that this was the sort of thing we usually did together.

"Mrs. Cornwall is donating stuff from her bakery, so I'm all set."

Lina smiled brightly. "See, I told you she likes you!"

Did she? I still wasn't sure. But she was willing to help, and that was all that mattered.

"I'll help out if you need me," Avangeline said.

"Actually, you guys can be my first customers! I'll be set up by eleven. Come by then?"

If everything went to plan, I'd be set up by ten-thirty and have a line by eleven. I'd chat people up and move slowly to make sure there was a wait. And once her parents were there, maybe they'd fall back in love themselves, or they'd eat the cake and then get back together and everything would be fixed.

"We definitely will," Avangeline said. "But are you sure you're okay, Emmie? You seem . . . off. And I know you'd hoped . . . I'm sorry I was so . . . They just . . ."

"Hey, it's okay." I rested my hand on her shoulder, because it really was okay. Now that I had a love spell cake, everything would be fine by tomorrow.

She smiled a shaky smile, and I tucked a curl behind her ear.

"I think we both just need a good bike ride and a swim," I said.

"Well, you're in luck, because I happen to be up for both those things." She moved her tank top to show off her tie-dye bathing suit.

"Okay, let me change, grab some stuff, and then we'll go," I said.

I grabbed the doorknob to go back inside.

"Wait, what happened there?" she asked.

I turned and, of course, there was the dead peach tree. In the middle of the lawn. Right where Avangeline could see it.

Think, think, think. How could I explain this?

"Another Mom casualty," I said.

Lina chuckled. "Moving the body before she gets back?"

"I was, and then I got . . . distracted." Distracted by the fact that my next-door neighbor was a witch.

I looked past Avangeline to Mrs. Cornwall's house. It was almost too much of a coincidence that the two last witches in town lived next to each other. And why had she been surprised I didn't know where magic came from? Where would I have learned that?

Avangeline touched my arm. "Where'd you go, Emmie?"

She smiled, but looked concerned.

"Just a lot running through my head. Sorry."

"That seems to happen a lot," she said. "Do you want to tell me about it?"

"Nah, it's just . . . stuff."

"It always is," she murmured. Then she shook her head. "Let me help you get the tree into the woods. It'll be easier with two of us."

We went down to the lawn and moved the tree together, sweating in the heat. Even though the dead tree wasn't that big, it was really heavy. Foot by foot we went, huffing and taking breaks until we got to the shade of the woods. My muscles ached by the time we dumped it.

I stared at the tree as I shook out my hands. If I'd used magic, I could've moved it in a second.

I paused, surprised by my own thought. For the first time since the dusting incident, I'd thought about how magic could make my life easier instead of harder, better instead of worse. I wasn't alone anymore, and with someone to guide me, my affinity for magic might turn out to be a good thing. Mrs. Cornwall had even called us unstoppable. I wasn't sure I wanted to be unstoppable, because that would mean people wanted us to stop. But for now all that mattered was that Avangeline would stay.

16

After I dropped my phone on Mrs. Cornwall's porch, Avangeline and I took the long way to the woods. The bike ride felt good even with the heat. The sun beat down on me, but the wind just about dried my sweat.

As soon as we got to our swimming spot, we cannonballed right into the Keeble. The icy water was a shock at first, but the cold was exactly what I needed.

I swam around, then treaded water in the deeper, middle part of the river.

"The one who stays under the longest is a mermaid!" Lina said.

I made a face but took a deep breath before going under. I may have had powers, but holding my breath wasn't one of them, so Avangeline almost always won. But I still tried.

I went under, opening my eyes and looking at the water and wavy sunlight above me. After around a minute, my lungs couldn't take it anymore. I surfaced, taking a big gulp of air. No Avangeline in sight. I looked into the river, and there she was, just chilling out in a little Zen pose.

She surfaced a whole twenty seconds later, her hair plastered to her head.

"Mermaid," I said.

She grinned and did a fist pump before splashing me. I splashed her right back, and we had a long splash battle in the shallower part of the river where our feet could touch the bottom.

We spent a while disappearing under the surface or sunning on the boulders as water rushed by. She sang, and I joined her in the parts I couldn't ruin with my lousy voice. Whenever we'd get hot we'd dive back in the river again. Or, well . . . I would dive.

There was a little cliff that hung, like, ten feet over a deep spot—it was our favorite jump-off. I'd put my hands over my head and dive in. Avangeline held her nose and jumped feetfirst. Despite being a great swimmer, she'd failed swim team because no matter how hard she tried, she couldn't make herself go headfirst at the water.

Okay, so she was a little bit of a chicken. But there was nothing wrong with being careful.

Hours and hours passed by in the blink of an eye.

I'd had a late breakfast, and we'd grabbed a bunch of snacks before we left my house, but we were down to peanut butter crackers and grossly warm juice pouches as we sat on our towels.

"It's so nice out," Avangeline said. "Such a perfect day for this."

"It is." I went to lean back, but I stopped myself because I wanted to look her in the eye. "I'm glad you stopped by."

"Me too. I really thought you might've been upset." She frowned, glancing to the side.

"Why'd you think that?" I asked.

"Well, I woke up and you were gone, and you don't normally do that."

"You're a late riser," I said.

She grinned. "Guilty. It really is cool, though—what you're going to do for Miss Sophia."

I nodded, even though my stomach twisted from not telling her the whole truth. But telling anyone the whole truth wasn't really possible in Samsonville. Except for Mrs. Cornwall.

"Anything new happen with your parents today?" I asked.

Avangeline shook her head. "No. They just avoided each other this morning, and then she went to the clinic." She paused, then took a deep breath. "Are you sure you're okay with the bracelet tap? I wouldn't have done it if . . . It's hard to explain."

"Lina, it's okay," I said. "That's the whole thing with the tap—you don't have to explain."

She smiled and placed her hand on top of mine. Our fingers were still cold and pruned from the river, but I loved the feeling of us connected while sitting apart. But then I realized I loved it too much. I was happy. And that could lead to my powers coming out in front of her.

I pulled my hand away. "Dragonfly," I said as one floated in the air in front of us.

Avangeline stared at our separated hands before looking away and pursing her lips.

"It's a blue dasher," she finally said.

Avangeline knew all about the wildlife by the Keeble. The woods were her second home, and now I had a way to let her keep them.

"You must be dreading the move," I said.

Lina's eyes darted away. "I'm not totally dreading it."

"What?" I shook my head to clear water out of my ear, because I couldn't have heard her right. And she'd spoken so softly, I wasn't sure I had.

I turned my body to face her head-on.

"I don't want to leave you or my dad, but it'll be nice to be with my other family more. My cousins and aunts." Her voice was barely above a whisper, and she still wasn't looking at me.

"Oh. Yeah, I guess that's good," I said.

"And New Orleans is . . ." She trailed off, then shook

her head. Finally, she met my eye and forced a smile. "Want the last cracker?"

She held out the pack, but I waved it off.

"New Orleans is what?" I asked.

She set it down, not eating it either, although she played with the wrapper. "It's a . . . fun place."

I stared at her, just blinking. A fun place. Not a place she was dreading or an okay place or just where some of her family lived. No, a fun place.

I backed up a few inches. Fun. New Orleans, where she'd never see me again, was fun. An arrow to my heart would've hurt less. We'd just had a great day biking and swimming and jumping off the cliff. But I guess that wasn't *fun* to her.

Shocked, I put my knees up to my chest and wrapped my arms around myself. I waited for her to take it back, but she didn't.

"Well, I guess any place is more fun than Samsonville." I grabbed a clump of grass and held it. But then I worried my powers would kill it, so I let go. I needed to stay calm, even if her words hurt.

Avangeline looked me in the eyes and sighed. "Emmie . . . no, don't be like this."

"Like what?"

"Upset. I didn't mean anything by that. I love Samsonville—you know that. This is where I've lived my whole life. But I hope when you visit New Orleans, we can do fun things together, that's all."

Yes, I was upset. And now for a brand-new reason.

"Sure. A visit would be great, when we can see each other here anytime just by riding our bikes."

"I know it's far, but—"

"And I'm sure my parents can just pay hundreds of dollars for a plane ticket for me whenever."

We didn't talk about money, but sometimes Avangeline didn't understand what it was like to not have a three-car garage or a brand-new bike or the latest cool sneakers or whatever.

"We'll figure something out," she said. "I can save up."

"That's generous."

It was generous, but not the way I said it. I plucked a weed and tore it apart.

We sat in silence. And the quieter we stayed, the more upset I became. How had we gotten on such different pages? Here I was scheming left and right to make her stay, and meanwhile, she was thinking New Orleans was fun.

Then the pieces started falling into place. The dinner the night before. The bracelet tap. How she'd done that despite us barely trying.

"Just say it. You're excited to go," I said. "You *want* to move to New Orleans."

I held my breath, waiting for her to respond.

Deny it. Just deny it and say you want to stay. Say you don't want to leave me behind.

She stared at me, her hazel eyes sad. "I know I'm going to have to."

That . . . wasn't denying it.

It felt like something I needed broke apart in my hand. This whole time I'd thought she wanted to stay, when really she was fine with going. And the worst part was she hadn't even had the courage to tell me that to my face.

Flame lit up my arms, itching under my skin. But, no. I would not, could not, let fire out. I exhaled, steadying myself. No powers. No magic. I would *not* lose control of my anger or cause anything to catch fire. If Avangeline didn't want to be here with me, then she should just go. Or I should.

I stood and grabbed my towel, yanking it off the ground. She stared up at me.

"Well, it's good you'll be leaving soon, then," I said.

She shook her head. "Emmie, stop. That's not what I said."

I took a step away, and then I spun on my heel, my bare feet tearing into the grass. "Why didn't you tell me?"

"Tell you what?"

"We watched all those movies. We made a whole list. We came up with a plan to get your parents back together, when the entire time you were fine with going. So why didn't you just say that?"

She frowned. "Emmie, I didn't want to hurt your feelings, and I—"

"I'm not a baby." I folded my arms like a grown-up, even though all I wanted to do was cry and throw a tantrum.

"I didn't say you were. I just mean . . . I don't know. Ugh, none of this is coming out right!" She stood up and slapped her sides. Her teeth bit her bottom lip as she stared up at the sky. She took a deep breath and then set her shoulders. "I thought if I said that there were some good things in New Orleans, that would seem like I didn't want to be here with you. And now that's what you think. And this is the worst. I shouldn't have said anything."

The worst. Now talking to me was *the worst.*

Hurt swirled in my chest like a million paper cuts. I was having a harder and harder time keeping it in check, but nothing good was going to come from releasing that feeling. Buzzing filled my head. What if I called in a swarm of bees or wasps? An insect swarm had happened once when Lina wanted to see fireflies on a night there weren't any—way too many had answered my call.

My pulse throbbed in my neck, each beat telling me I needed to get out of there and quickly, because no matter how much she was hurting me, I couldn't hurt Avangeline.

I hurried and put my sandals on and tipped my bike upright. "It's fine, Avangeline."

She took a few steps closer with her hand out. "No, it's not. Emmie, wait—"

"It's getting late."

"No, it isn't."

"It's fine."

"It's not. Don't just leave. Talk to me. Don't run away."

"Don't even come tomorrow."

I got on my bike and pedaled away. I was already a mile from the Keeble before my first tear fell.

17

I rode all around town, careful to avoid thinking about anything too much. Instead, I focused on the wind wrapping around me. The burn in my leg muscles. Anything other than my feelings. I had to stay calm and neutral, even though my heart was breaking, because whatever control I had earlier was gone.

Yes, I could've run home and been safe, but I didn't want to. If I was home, I'd have to talk to Oliver and Persimmon and try to explain what had happened at Mrs. Cornwall's, and I didn't have the energy for all that.

So I rode my bike.

I passed the abandoned warehouses and factories on the outskirts of town, with their boarded-up doors and broken windows. Samsonville had had almost ten thousand people at one point, but things had changed.

Businesses had closed and people had moved away. A lot of Upstate New York was like that. A lot of life was like that, I guessed—things changed for the worse, and people left or wanted to. I just never thought that would include Avangeline.

The sun got lower and lower until I had to head home. It was going to get dark, and my parents might've checked on me, even though I'd texted before I left. Still, I pedaled slowly, in no rush to get to Mrs. Cornwall's. I didn't want to talk to her, but maybe I could say I was just exhausted and head to bed. Which was true. It had been one of the longest days ever.

I grabbed my overnight bag off my front porch where I'd left it that morning and walked to Mrs. Cornwall's house. I knocked on the door, but there was no answer. Confused, I knocked again, until I noticed the note taped to the door. In perfect script, Mrs. Cornwall had written that she needed to run errands and would be back late, with a reminder that we had church in the morning.

I peeled off the note. On the back there was a second note saying there was a key under the welcome mat. I grabbed my phone from the steps and unlocked the door, glad to be alone.

Until I walked in.

Turned out, it was super strange to be all by myself in someone else's house at night. Especially someone I knew was a witch. The grandfather clock chimed an off-key sound as I went by. I smelled something cooking, so I went down the hall to the huge kitchen. On top of one of the stoves was a chicken pot pie with a note for me to help myself. It smelled good, but I wasn't in the mood to eat. Instead, I felt an overwhelming urge to be nosy.

I continued through the kitchen and noticed a study to the left. I went in. (In my defense, the office door was open, so it wasn't like I picked the lock.)

Mrs. Cornwall had bookcases and a desk, and just like the rest of her house, everything was pristine. There was a shallow bowl with perfect flowers floating in it and just enough papers and pens on the desk to make it look like someone very neat worked there.

I went behind her desk, and I couldn't help but touch some of the old books. Okay, I kind of thought a secret passageway would open up if I pulled the right one, but nothing happened. There was one book in particular on the middle shelf that looked out of place. It was titled *Malleus Maleficarum*.

I'd just picked it up when there was a loud creaking above me, like someone stomping angrily on the second floor. I jumped and nearly dropped the old book. I waited, clutching the book to my chest, heart pounding, expecting someone to come charging at me. Only . . . there was no one. I was alone.

Trying to slow my heart, I glanced around. After a scare like that, there should've been books floating or papers swirling or something askew on the desk. But . . . nothing had happened. This wasn't a coincidence. For some reason, I didn't have magic in this house.

I was back to being normal—the thing I'd wanted for so long.

A cold chill rushed through me, and I hugged the book tighter. I was confused until I remembered this feeling. I was *scared*, for the first time in years. I was frightened because I *didn't* have magic.

I'd never thought of my powers as something that helped me. They were always something to fear. I hadn't realized that the reason I'd been brave was because my powers were always there for me to use. And now without them I felt . . . exposed.

I shuddered and rushed to put the book back. It was time to get out of the study. I needed to calm down and stop snooping. But the other books crowded in. I grunted and had to shove the unruly books aside to get the volume back in.

I went up the stairs, and each wooden step groaned. I wasn't sure how old this house was, but it was probably over a hundred years old, like Aunt Catherine's house. So the creaking I'd heard in the office was probably just an old home being weird. Still, for some reason, it felt like the house didn't want me there. Which was ridiculous, since houses didn't have opinions.

Except, mine did. So maybe hers did too.

And this one didn't like me.

Upstairs there were five doors. The doors to a bathroom and one bedroom were open—where I was supposed to shower and sleep. Two were closed, and one slammed shut just as I got to the top of the steps.

I lingered in the hall, even though I knew where I *should* go. The other rooms were probably shut for a reason, but why? What was she hiding? And why had that last door suddenly closed?

I took a step toward that doorknob, but in my head I heard Avangeline screaming at me to not be the first girl to die in a horror movie. If I had my powers, I would've checked anyhow, but since I didn't, I backed up. Instead of investigating, I went into the open bedroom and tossed my bag down. It was a nice enough room, with a full-size bed, dresser, and a mirror in the corner. Everything looked old and varnished, but there wasn't a speck of dust.

For a minute I sat on the bed and waited, listening. I wasn't sure what I expected, but there was just the normal sound of crickets at night. Eventually, I grabbed my hairbrush and toothbrush and went into the bathroom.

The warm shower made me feel worlds better. As I washed off the river, I tried to rinse away what had happened with Avangeline, but it clung to me. Doubt started to seep in as I conditioned my hair. Maybe I'd overreacted. Maybe I hadn't let her talk, since I'd cut her off a few times. She always said her parents talked over her. But no. I'd listened. I'd heard every word of how New Orleans would be fun and I was being a baby about it.

Okay, that wasn't word for word what she'd said, but it was what she'd meant.

And then the water went from hot to ice-cold.

I turned the knobs frantically, but it didn't help. Freezing, I had to hurry out, conditioner still globbed in my hair.

I grabbed my towel and rinsed my hair in the sink. Once I finished, I wiped the fog off the mirror. Only, when I looked, I didn't have a reflection. There was just the wall behind me—like I was invisible.

My scream was so loud the walls shook. I looked again, and there I was, pale as ever and totally freaked out.

What the heck was that?

I set the world speed record for brushing my teeth, then went into the bedroom and closed the door. I changed into pajamas and brushed my hair in the room, pacing around.

That was . . . freaky.

I thought about packing up my stuff and leaving. My parents could ground me if they wanted; I wasn't staying at Mrs. Cornwall's—not when the house didn't want me there.

But no. If I left, my parents would come home immediately. And despite everything, I still wanted to have the bake sale the next day. Maybe I was overreacting to all of this. Old pipes ran cold, floors creaked, shelves slanted. I was beyond exhausted and cranky. Still, I shot a glance over to the mirror in the corner to be sure. There I was, with wet hair and wild eyes, looking frazzled.

After pacing around for about a mile, I finally got into bed. Nothing bad had actually happened to me. I was just on edge and freaked out. I mean, I'd learned today that my neighbor was a witch with an enchanted bakery. It had been far from a normal day. I checked my phone—nothing from Avangeline. I sighed and texted my parents that I was going to bed early.

Eventually, I made myself get under the quilt. All of my muscles were tired, my heart was heavy, and my mind was full. I needed to get some rest. Maybe everything would be better in the morning.

I wasn't thrilled with turning my light off, but the hallway light was bright under the door. It was so weird to be afraid of the dark for the first time. Now I finally understood how Avangeline felt—scared of what might be lurking and powerless to stop it. That was why she was so nervous all the time. It would've been awful to feel this helpless. Maybe she felt the same way about the move to New Orleans. Powerless to stop it, so she might as well accept it. But she wouldn't have to go. I'd make sure of it.

I picked up my phone to text her, but I stopped typing. She needed to text me first, since I was the one hurting. And it wasn't like I could tell her I finally understood why she was so cautious. I put my phone back on the nightstand with a sigh, and then I tossed and turned. But somehow, between the soft bed and the long day, I started drifting off to sleep. In fact, I was almost out when I heard a scream.

My eyes shot open, and I sat up and looked around. Heart pounding, clutching the quilt, and now very much awake, I fumbled for the light. There was nothing in my room. I got up and went to the door. Normally, I would've thrown it open and explored, but instead, I carefully cracked it open just enough for one eye to see out. There was nothing in the hall.

It had sounded like the scream was coming from right by my door, but I looked around, and there was nothing out of the ordinary. Just the bright light and the bathroom door open. I went into the hall and then stuck my head into the bathroom, and it was empty. The mirror reflected me like normal.

I stood still for a second, every muscle tense, waiting for another sound, another scream. My hands were ready in front of me like I could defend myself, even though I knew I couldn't. But there was just the sound of me breathing heavily. Had I imagined the scream? Was it one of those weird things where I'd thought I was awake but I was really asleep?

I went back into my room and locked the door. I decided I'd sleep with the light on. Just in case.

18

I didn't get the best night's sleep, and I wasn't at my most awake for church the next morning. Every few minutes in the pew, I felt my eyelids get heavy and my head bob, but then I'd get a very displeased look from Mrs. Cornwall. Seriously, though, how long were services? It felt like we'd been in church for hours. And it was only 8:52 a.m.

I took out my phone to try to wake myself up. Also because I was super bored.

"Absolutely not," Mrs. Cornwall whispered sharply. She wore a skirt suit and a stern expression—like an angry politician.

I wasn't sure why God would care if I played *Mario Kart*, but I put it away.

After about an eon (9:30 a.m.), services were finally

over. Mrs. Cornwall and I walked down the center aisle. And there, right outside the door, were Avangeline and her family.

I thought about going past her, since she still hadn't messaged, but Mrs. Cornwall came to a stop in front of Dr. Monroe.

"Good morning," Mrs. Cornwall said. "Beautiful service."

"Yes, it was," Dr. Monroe replied. She stood with Max and Avangeline. Mr. Monroe was off talking to Mr. Miles. Everyone was dressed up except for me. The spare shorts and shirt I kept in my overnight bag looked extra ratty next to them.

I caught Avangeline looking at me, but I pretended like I hadn't seen it.

"Will we see you at the picnic later? It's the perfect day for Founder's Day," Mrs. Cornwall said.

"Oh, I think I may have to miss this year. I have a bad case that might need surgery at the clinic," Dr. Monroe said.

No.

Panic rose inside me, and I dug my short nails into my palms to try to calm down. I wasn't totally sure I wanted to give her the cake, but if she didn't come, I wouldn't even have the option.

"I thought we were going," Avangeline said quietly.

"Your father can take you." Dr. Monroe glanced over at Mr. Monroe, and she didn't smile.

No. No. No. She was the one who had to eat the cake. What was I going to do? I opened my mouth, but I wasn't sure what to say. I closed my lips, and it made a strange sound—like a fish.

Mrs. Cornwall side-eyed me. "That's too bad. I made a special red velvet cake for Emma's bake sale today. It's cooling right now, as a matter of fact."

Dr. Monroe hesitated. "Oh, that's right. Avangeline mentioned the fundraiser. Maybe I —"

"You should stop by, and then you can go to the clinic right after," I said. "I'll be setting up soon!"

It came out loud and rushed and high-pitched. In short: really, really weird. Mrs. Cornwall, Dr. Monroe, and Avangeline all turned and stared at me. Even Max tilted his head. Avangeline's mood ring turned orange. She was probably confused about why I was being such a weirdo.

"You did promise Max you'd go for a little while," Avangeline said. "And next year . . ." She trailed off and frowned.

Dr. Monroe nodded, then looked at her watch. "All right. I can probably spare half an hour."

"Awesome!" I said.

Mrs. Cornwall quirked an eyebrow at me. I wanted to tell her that my weirdness was mostly her fault, since I hadn't gotten a good night's sleep thanks to her super-creepy house. But it wasn't like I could say that in front of everyone. And my parents would've punished me until the end of time for being that rude.

"Okay, we'll see you there," Mrs. Cornwall said. "Come along, Emma."

We walked away, and I looked back over my shoulder. I was just in time to catch Avangeline doing the same thing. We locked eyes, and she gave me a little smile and my heart filled. With just one glance, I knew that even though we weren't really talking, I couldn't let her leave.

I followed Mrs. Cornwall back to her Subaru and got into the passenger seat. It was odd to see her buckle into a car like a normal person when I knew she could make plates float and books disappear.

"You have to learn to be more subtle, Emma," Mrs. Cornwall said, at the same time I asked, "Do witches really ride broomsticks?"

So much for subtle.

She sighed at me as she started the car. "Yes, they did a long time ago, when people used to travel by horse. Cars and planes are safer and faster than trying to balance on a broomstick. They're also far less noticeable. But there are spells to do it in a pinch."

She reversed out of her parking spot as I tried to imagine balancing on a floating broom. Maybe it was easier than I thought, since . . . magic.

"Is the love cake really ready?" I asked.

I hadn't seen one in the kitchen before we ran out the door in the morning. Mrs. Cornwall insisted we get to the church half an hour early—like we needed front-row tickets or something. When we got there, I realized that she just liked to talk to people before services started. You would've thought she was the mayor of Samsonville, with how many people came up to say hi. But it wasn't a surprise, since everyone always commented on how great she was.

"Yes, we're going to Collingsworth's now to get it," Mrs. Cornwall said.

That made sense. All of her industrial baking equipment was there. I'd just assumed she'd bake the cake in her house.

"That's where I was last night," she added.

I shuddered, my shoulders shimmying as I remembered the scream before bed. I never figured out what it was. It was probably just the house messing with me. But houses couldn't scream—even ones that belonged to witches. At least . . . I didn't think so.

We arrived at Collingsworth's and parked in the back.

"I still need to frost the cake and take care of a few things in the store," Mrs. Cornwall said.

"Oh, I'll just wait here, then, if it's okay," I said.

She nodded and opened her door. "I assume you'll also need a folding table, plates, and a cashbox, too, for the bake sale."

I pursed my lips. I hadn't thought about any of that. "Yes, ma'am."

"It's all right, Emma. Like I said, we need to take care of each other."

She smiled and I nodded. She was right—she was helping me, even if I felt strange about her house or how I couldn't say anything about her secret.

As I waited alone in the car, I texted my parents, letting them know we were done with church. They said they were just sitting down to breakfast and would leave right after. Earlier than I hoped, but I still had over three hours until they got back. It wasn't a ton of time, but it was enough.

I switched over to *Mario Kart* and tried to focus, but my eyelids felt heavy and the sun was in my face. I leaned the seat back to get more comfortable. Then I rested my eyes for just a second.

"Wake up, little witch," Mrs. Cornwall said. She'd opened the back of her car.

I startled awake and nearly flung myself out of my seat. I put my hands up to defend myself, power flowing through me, but just managed to stop myself from letting it out.

"A little jumpy, aren't we?" she said. The corner of her lips turned up.

"Sorry, I must've fallen asleep." I rubbed my face, and then I realized I'd been asleep for a while, because my mouth felt dry and I was rested. I looked at the clock. Forty-five minutes had gone by since we'd parked.

"Oh no!" I said.

"What's wrong?"

"It's been almost an hour. What if Dr. Monroe already came and went? What if we missed her? What will we do then?"

"Emma, calm down," Mrs. Cornwall said. "I'm sure she hasn't even gotten to the park yet. Almost everyone changes after church. And the picnic doesn't start for another fifteen minutes. But if you'd like to move this along, come help me load everything into the back."

I hopped out of the car and helped arrange things in the trunk, including a two-layer red velvet cake in a see-through cake box. The cake was beautiful and smelled amazing. As I stared at the intricate rose-petal design and red sprinkles over cream cheese frosting, I realized why it had taken her so long in the bakery. This wasn't me quickly spreading chocolate frosting over yellow cake on Mother's Day.

"Is that it?" I asked.

She looked at me like it was a ridiculous question. "Yes."

"So if Dr. Monroe eats this, she'll fall back in love?" I pointed to the cake.

Apparently, I had nothing but ridiculous questions. It was just hard to believe that there was a love spell cake sitting in the back of a Subaru.

"Yes. Would you like to try a piece?" Mrs. Cornwall gestured to the cake box.

"It . . . it won't make me fall in love?"

She shook her head. "No, that's not how it works."

So the cake would only affect Dr. Monroe? I had so much to learn about potions.

We finished getting the folding table in and closed the trunk. Then we took the short drive to Bryan Park.

Time to make Avangeline's parents fall back in love.

19

Bryan Park was a green space with playgrounds, sports fields, and a big lawn that bordered the Keeble. The picnic would be on the lawn at eleven o'clock. Some families had already staked out their spots, unfurling their blankets. The people who'd volunteered to grill were lighting them up, and the scent of charcoal filled the air. The band was setting up on the stage, playing random notes for sound check.

Of course, everyone said hello to Mrs. Cornwall as we arrived. Mr. Hollis and Old Mr. Day came over and helped us get everything out of the car. Old Mr. Day, our only regular at Occult & Davidson, owned Morrisey's ice cream stand. Mr. Hollis was the town historian and kind of looked like the guy on KFC buckets. He ran the

Museum of Witchery. He grinned at Mrs. Cornwall, hoping for her to look his way.

Then it dawned on me that even though everyone called her "Mrs. Cornwall" and she wore a wedding ring, I'd never met a Mr. Cornwall, and my parents had never mentioned him.

"Are you married?" I asked once we were alone.

We were on opposite ends of the folding table, laying out a tablecloth.

"Are you going to ask odd questions all day?" she said.

"I'm sorry . . . I was just thinking about how everyone calls you Missus, but I haven't met your husband."

She looked down her nose at me. "You really don't know enough about this town's history, do you? The reason the women in the bakery were suspected to begin with was that they were older than twenty-one and had never married. Women who don't conform to society's expectations are always suspect."

"Oh."

She laid out napkins in a circle. "You'll see. You're still a girl, so you're allowed to be different, but society will close in around you as soon as you get to be a woman."

I had no idea what to say to that, and she didn't seem like she wanted a reply. Instead, I looked for Avangeline's family again. More and more people were arriving, and it was hard to check every blanket and lawn chair, so I focused on setting up the display of cookies, muffins, cupcakes, and a carrot cake. Mrs. Cornwall had even loaned me a Collingsworth's banner. I hung it in the trees behind the table. We put out everything except the red velvet cake. That I stored under the table, where it would stay cool. I wanted to make sure there would be a big slice for Dr. Monroe. And whether it was magic or just cake decorating, no one could keep their eyes off the red velvet cake as we walked it through the lawn.

"All right, I think we're all set," Mrs. Cornwall said. "I'm going to go home and change. I'll be by later."

"Thanks for all your help. I couldn't have done this without you," I said.

"Like I told you, Emma, we have to help each other. Try to remember that."

She walked away, and I stood behind the table with the distinct feeling that she still didn't like me. She also hadn't answered my question about having a husband—my guess was she didn't.

About a minute later, I stopped wondering because I had my first customer. After that I was just busy. I greeted each person with a smile and wished them a happy Founder's Day and asked how their summer was going. Soon, even without trying, I had a long line. People were generous with donating for the library, and as usual, everyone was raving about Mrs. Cornwall's baking.

And then the person I'd been waiting for appeared in front of me with a smile.

"Am I too late for the cake?" Dr. Monroe said, scanning the table.

"No. I have it right here." I took the box out from under the table, to some *oohs* and *ahhs*.

"Why weren't we offered that?" Isabella's mom, Mrs. Miles, said. She'd just bought a muffin and a cupcake and had taken two steps away. She had her normal sour look on her face, like she'd just smelled expired milk.

"There wasn't room on the table," I said. It wasn't a total lie, since I had to take away the empty carrot cake tray to fit the cake box.

I took the lid off and realized Mrs. Cornwall had already cut the cake into eight slices. Apparently, no one trusted me with a knife.

But it did make serving easier. I carefully removed two slices of the super-moist cake and put them on plates. It looked delicious. I didn't even like her cakes, and something in me wanted to devour it.

"Wow, that is so beautiful," Dr. M. said. "Mrs. Cornwall outdid herself."

I was hoping that Mr. Monroe would be in line with her, but that hadn't worked out.

"You should take one for Mr. Monroe too," I said. "Before we sell out—on me."

"Hmm, okay," Dr. Monroe said. "I'll also take a

couple of these cookies for the kids. What do I owe you, dear?"

"It's pay-what-you-will to benefit the library."

"Well, then keep it all," she said, handing me two twenties.

"Wow, thanks, Dr. M." I opened up the cashbox and put the money inside.

She put the cookies in her purse, and then I handed her the cake plates. My chest filled with hope, like butterfly wings beating. Maybe it would really work. And then Avangeline would stay.

Fall in love. Just fall back in love.

Dr. Monroe smiled and walked away with the plates, and lonely Mr. Haywood was next. Mr. Haywood was my dad's age, but he was always walking by himself or eating alone and muttering to himself. He was an author or something.

"I'll take a slice too. That looks too good to pass up," he said.

I served cake to him, then to Miss Sophia, the librarian, who was in a long pink dress that made her look even more like Belle. The next slice went to old Mrs. Antonio, and one to Old Mr. Day. The last two slices went to Mr. Miles, who'd gotten back in line. The cake was gone within three minutes of me putting it out. I was really glad I'd hidden it under the table, or it would've been sold before Dr. M got in line. And that would've been a disaster.

After a few more customers, everything was gone. All around me, everyone was talking about how good the food was, and people kept coming over hoping I had something left. I wasn't sure how Mrs. Cornwall enchanted her food, but it worked. A small part of me wondered if it would work on my parents' store. They really did need the customers.

I started cleaning up, taking the banner down and throwing out the trash. I looked for Mrs. Cornwall, but she was nowhere to be found. Then again, with hundreds of people on the lawn and the band starting, she could've been anywhere.

As I scanned the crowd, I noticed something weird. Mr. and Mrs. Miles, whose blanket was nearby, weren't fighting. In fact, they were *snuggling*. Isabella was sitting next to them, looking like she wanted to throw up or disappear. So that was . . . weird and gross. I gave her a sympathetic shrug, and she sighed, smiling at me a little, like she preferred it when they were arguing.

By the evergreen trees to the left side of the lawn, Old Mr. Day was talking to Mrs. Antonio. They looked happy, and it made me smile. They'd both lost their spouses recently, and they seemed like they needed company. Mr. Day started fanning Mrs. Antonio with his hat, probably because the sun had started to make it warm on the lawn.

I looked toward the river, trying to spot Mrs. Cornwall. That's when I noticed lonely Mr. Haywood was kneeling on Miss Sophia's gingham blanket, and she was blushing and giggling. I stared for a second, because Miss Sophia was not a giggler. Then again, Founder's Day put everyone in a good mood. And it was nice to see Mr. Haywood actually talking to someone other than himself.

Then, in the distance, I finally saw Avangeline's family. She and her parents were in the back of the crowd, watching Max running around. Suddenly, Dr. Monroe reached up and took Mr. Monroe's chin in her hand. Then she kissed him. Actually kissed him on the mouth!

I blinked hard, not believing my own eyes. But no, she was still kissing him!

It had to have been the cake. She'd eaten it and fallen back in love with her husband. They'd get back together. Avangeline would stay in town.

Celebration lit through me. I took a deep breath, trying to tamp it down. I could've made the fireworks go off early, with the amount of joy I felt. I had to stay contained. Neutral.

A wave of anger rose in me as happiness faded. It wasn't fair that I couldn't let myself celebrate, even when the one thing I wanted more than anything had just happened.

I looked around for someone to talk to, but I couldn't tell anyone about my success. It didn't matter, though, since everyone was busy. Avangeline was playing with Max in the distance. Isabella was on her phone, ignoring her parents, who were making out, and Miss Sophia was staring with goo-goo eyes at Mr. Haywood.

And then it hit me. The love potion had worked *too* well.

Oh my God.

Everyone who'd eaten the cake was falling in love.

20

No, no, no.

I kept staring at the four couples, and each time I looked, it was somehow getting worse. Mr. Miles was feeding Mrs. Miles off his fork as she made kissy faces at him. Mr. Haywood was dramatically reciting a poem to Miss Sophia, who was still giggling. Then he accidentally knocked her over and she fell down, laughing. Old Mr. Day was tucking a flower into Mrs. Antonio's white hair. And Dr. Monroe and Mr. Monroe had started slow-dancing to the band.

No, no, no. This wasn't supposed to happen! Well, except for Avangeline's parents. That was good. But the rest of this *definitely* was not.

I scanned the crowd, desperately hoping to find Mrs. Cornwall. Had she somehow messed up the potion so it affected anyone who ate the cake? Maybe she didn't even know she'd screwed up, since she'd offered me a slice earlier. But no, she'd specifically said it wouldn't work on other people.

Wait. No. She'd said it wouldn't work on *me*—a witch. No! Maybe I wasn't supposed to give it to anyone else. Why didn't she tell me that??

In my head, I heard the answer: she didn't think I'd be foolish enough to give it to anyone else. Seeing as it was literally a magic fall-in-love cake.

Panic swirled in my chest. There were eight people in love, and six were a big problem.

All of a sudden, a gust of wind blew through the park. People grabbed at plates and napkins, and my long hair floated on the stiff breeze. No. No. No. I was not going to call in a windstorm on top of everything else. I needed to get home. Now. Regroup and figure out how to fix all this.

I closed up the cashbox and looked around for my bike, and then I remembered Mrs. Cornwall had driven me there. I'd have to walk all the way home. I tipped my head back in frustration, and that's when Avangeline appeared next to me.

"Hi, Emma," she said.

"Avangeline." I tried to control my breathing. No wind. Calm skies. Stay neutral. Unfortunately, it felt like I was in the eye of a tornado. Where I stood was fine, but all around me I could feel my powers swirling, ready to go out of control. I needed an excuse to get out of there.

She came closer. So close I could smell the apple scent of her hair. "I'm really sorry about what I said yesterday. At the river."

"I know. I am too," I said. "And it's all okay. But I really need to go."

She shook her head, looking sad. "Please don't."

"I have to. I promise it doesn't have anything to do with you. I swear."

"Emma, please wait." She let out a big sigh. "You always do this. You run away when I try to talk to you about real things."

"I don't always—I just have to this time."

"I love you."

Suddenly, everything around me went quiet. All I could feel was the wild beating of my heart. She loved me.

Avangeline wasn't the type of person who just said she loved someone. I wasn't sure if she meant she loved me as a friend or what, but she'd never said that either. I stared at her, and her hazel eyes were sincere. She loved me, and I loved her. Who knew what kind of love it was, but it didn't really matter. She loved me. She didn't want to just leave me behind.

I forgot about my panic. Everyone else at Founder's

Day disappeared. All I saw was the constellation of Avangeline's freckles. I gathered a breath: I'd tell her. I'd tell her I loved her too.

And I was just about to say it when I noticed a little speck of red by her mouth.

A red sprinkle.

21

No.

No, no, no.

"You, um . . . you didn't eat any cake just now, did you?" I asked.

Avangeline nodded enthusiastically. "Yeah, I had some of my dad's cake. It was delicious!"

Noooooo.

Oh God. No. Not Avangeline. I was the worst person in the world. I belonged in jail for making my best friend think she was in love with me.

Because she wasn't.

I should never have gone through with the love spell. What had I been *thinking*?

I let out a whimper, then ran out of the park. I had to get home and fix this NOW, and I had no idea how to do it. I heard Avangeline call my name, but I didn't look back. As I left the park, grill flames exploded high behind me. The cooks jumped back, exclaiming.

You're the worst, Emma. Awful, Emma. Terrible, foolish clown girl.

What would I do now?

I ran over Holy Cross Bridge, the river level rising and falling with each of my breaths. I really wished I had my bike to get home faster. But I focused on sprinting as hard as I could. Coins jingled in the cashbox, and I tried not to notice streetlamps burning bright as I passed them . . . in broad daylight. Anyone driving down the road could've seen them flicker on and off as I ran. Just incident after incident.

Oh God. I really hoped my parents weren't back yet. There was no way I could explain all of this.

I ran even faster. I had to make it home before them.

This was the biggest disaster of my life. Easily. Hands-down winner. I had made a bunch of people fall in love by accident, including my best friend. That was way worse than exploding Carmichael.

I needed to find some kind of antidote, quick, before anyone figured it out . . . but it wasn't like there were tons of anti–love spell antidotes just hanging around.

Wait. Maybe there were. Mrs. Cornwall could probably fix all of this—maybe without anyone ever knowing. She had a book of spells and knew how to make potions, and since she wasn't at the park, she was probably at her house.

I ran as fast as possible, trying not to notice the leaves changing from green to fire-engine red to green again as I went by. I got to Mrs. Cornwall's and banged on her door. Then I stooped over, trying to catch my breath. I had the worst side stitch of my life, and it felt like my heart had lodged into my throat. Like my pulse wanted to choke me.

There was no answer.

I rang the doorbell twice. I knocked again. I peered into all the windows. Nothing. No one was there.

Ugh. No! How was she not home?

A swirl of wind hit me, drying my sweat. It felt good until I realized it came from my powers. No! I could easily cause a natural disaster feeling like this.

I ran to my house, but I was halfway there before I remembered I'd locked the doors. And, ugh, no! The key was in my backpack. Which was in Mrs. Cornwall's house. Which was also locked.

Okay, okay, don't panic. There's a spare key to Mrs. Cornwall's.

I jogged back across and shifted the mat, but the key was gone. Because I'd taken it into the house and put it in the bowl by the door last night.

No. Not me being the valedictorian of Clown College.

Emotions swirled inside me. I couldn't get into my safe space. I couldn't stay neutral. What would I do? How would I deal with this?

But wait. Maybe I could command the front doors to open like Mrs. Cornwall had.

I ran back over and hopped up onto my front porch.

"Open," I said. I waved my hand at the doors, feeling ridiculous.

They didn't budge.

Dismayed, I stared. There had to be a way to do it, but I didn't exactly have time to learn right now.

I knocked on the glass of the shop door, hoping Oliver would be able to get it open from the inside, but neither pet answered. I'd really have to talk to them about their refusal to greet me.

I was about to try again when I heard wheels coming up the driveway. I spun around, and there was Avangeline riding up to the house.

No! How was I supposed to remain calm now? I needed to be alone, to just breathe and find a way back to my neutral zone.

She came to a stop and put out the kickstand.

"Emma, that was mean," she said.

I rubbed my face with my hands. "I know. I'm sorry, Lina. But I really need to be alone right now." I could feel the wind picking up around me.

"You literally ran away from me." She took off her bike helmet and clipped it onto her handlebar. She walked up to me and put her hands on her hips. I'd never seen her do that before. Lina wasn't the type of person to confront someone.

"Lina, I'm sorry. I really am. I just needed to go." My eyes darted to the clouds gathering overhead and then to the doors again.

"First you didn't listen to me, and then you ran away from me. What gives? I thought we cared about each other. I thought we were friends. I thought we . . . I don't know, but this is not cool." Her lips were a line, and her brow was furrowed.

I'd never seen her this angry, and there was real pain in my chest from causing it. But the more I felt, the worse things would get. I would probably call in a hurricane. There was a distinct whirling inside me, and the sky was mimicking what I felt, the clouds swirling. No. I had to get in the house or get her safely away from me. Only how?

"And you still don't want to be near me." She slapped her hand against her side. "You won't even look at me."

"It's not you. I swear. I'm just . . . I'm in a mess, and I need time to fix it."

Her eyes narrowed. "What happened?"

"I . . ." I couldn't tell her. I *physically* couldn't tell her about Mrs. Cornwall, but I couldn't tell her the rest of it either. None of it would make sense without revealing that I had powers. "There's too much to even know where to start."

I closed my mouth and looked away.

She waited, eyes scanning me. "That's it? All you have to say is 'there's too much'? You never talk to me. I tell you I love you, and you can't even tell me what's wrong?"

I cringed, thinking about that red sprinkle. "You don't love me, though. You just think you do."

The words sounded terrible and seemed to hang in the air.

"Are we even friends?" She stuck up her left wrist, the one with the friendship bracelet.

"Of course we are." I moved a couple steps closer to her.

"You really don't think I know how I feel?" she said.

Okay, so this was a pickle. She didn't know how she felt because I'd accidentally made her fall in love with me, but I couldn't tell her that, so I just settled for shaking my head, which was not a great response.

Avangeline looked at me, and her eyes got glassy. "You're acting just like my parents. They don't think I can handle the truth, but if they'd just talk to—"

"That's not true—" I interrupted.

"You can't even let me finish! You know I hate it when people talk over me. I thought you were different."

"Lina . . ."

"I can *feel* when you're not being honest." She pointed to her chest. "Are you being honest with me? Right now?"

"I'm . . ." No. I was a liar and a bad friend who didn't deserve her. "I'm as honest as I can be."

Her lip quivered as tears pooled in her eyes. She took a deep breath and then slid off the friendship bracelet. "Whatever. Take this back."

"Avangeline." I shook my head again and again. This couldn't be happening. Not this. Anything but this.

I wanted to scream. I wanted to beg for her to stay. I wanted to break down and explain how things had gone so horribly wrong.

But I couldn't lose control in front of her.

She stared at me, and I knew she was waiting for me to say something, anything. But what could I say? Avangeline was right. I'd been lying to her for years. I didn't really deserve to be her friend.

I stayed quiet, and she tossed the bracelet to the ground. The one I'd tied to a clipboard and knotted for hours. Because even back in fourth grade, I'd loved her in some kind of way. And now I loved her and wanted to spend every minute together, but I needed her to go. Before I hit the town with a tornado.

I watched the bracelet fall to the pavement, and it hurt. It really hurt. But it was okay—I deserved it. I closed my eyes and just accepted the sharp, stabbing pain in my heart.

Until Lina gasped.

My eyes shot open.

No! Had I hurt her somehow? But she wasn't looking

at me. Instead she was staring at the space next to the porch.

I glanced down. Four bloodred rosebushes had sprouted up, with thorns the size of kitchen knives.

The thorns would've been unusual enough, but there hadn't even been rosebushes in front of the house. Not before a second ago.

Avangeline looked at the flowers and then up at me. "Emmie . . . what just happened?"

I reached for a lie, a half-truth, but I was so tired of lying. It was what had gotten me into all this in the first place. "It's . . . it's part of a long story that I've never been able to tell you."

Avangeline blinked a few times and then swallowed hard. "Okay. I think you need to start from the beginning."

22

Avangeline was doing pretty well for someone who'd just found out that her best friend had magical powers. She'd perched on one of the rocking chairs in the back as I'd paced in front of her and told her everything. Well, everything except for Mrs. Cornwall's involvement, because I was still enchanted not to mention it.

I finished, and she was silent for a while.

"So you're . . . like, a superhero?" Avangeline said, dazed.

"I'm not even tall." I sighed. "I just have these . . . abilities. And they're not predictable. They go out of control, and then things happen like this and I scramble to fix it."

"Things like making a town and your best friend

fall in love and interfering with my parents even though you promised you wouldn't?"

"Yes, those parts."

I rubbed my forehead. It was a good sign that she hadn't run screaming or come at me with a pitchfork, I guessed.

"This is a lot." She blew out a breath.

"I know. I know it is, and I'm sorry to put it all out there like this," I said. "And I'm sorry I broke my promise to you."

She nodded and was silent for a beat again. "It must've been really hard for you. Keeping this a secret."

Me? After everything I'd told her, she was thinking about me? I didn't deserve her.

"I mean . . . it wasn't that hard, because no one would have believed me anyway." I stared at the ground.

She shrugged. "Maybe, but it's also incredible."

"Really?" My powers were many things—*incredible* wasn't usually how I described them.

"I mean . . . Emmie, you're an actual, real live magical being that can make a rosebush appear out of nowhere. That's beyond amazing!"

I . . . I'd never thought of it that way.

Avangeline's face glowed like she was happy for me. She hadn't run away. She didn't seem scared or disgusted or mad. She just accepted me.

A warmth I'd never felt before flooded through me,

and a ray of sunshine lit up the back porch. Lina's mouth opened, amazed.

I dug my thumb into my palm and took a deep breath, trying to calm down. The sunshine slowly faded back into shade.

Avangeline stared at my hand. She reached out and moved my thumb. "It's okay," she whispered.

The sunlight returned. She smiled and held my hand. Heat rushed through me from my toes to my forehead.

"I really am sorry, Lina," I said.

"I wish you could've told me earlier," she said. "It must've been really lonely, keeping all this inside because of your parents."

"They were just trying to protect me. They think this kind of power is dangerous, and . . . it is."

Avangeline nodded. "But you wouldn't use your powers to hurt people, because you're not like that."

No, I wasn't, but that didn't matter much. "Either way, it's dangerous, because if other people knew, they'd be afraid. And fear makes people do bad things."

Mrs. Cornwall also believed that, and she wasn't wrong. Jealousy and fear had led to the death of nearly all witches. Except us.

"I mean, maybe," Avangeline said. "You can't control what other people fear, though. For example, I'm afraid of everything, including possums that get stuck in the compost."

I smiled, despite everything that had happened.

"I'm glad you told me." She took my other hand.

"Thanks for not getting completely freaked out." I squeezed her hands and held on.

"Honestly, it explains a lot—a lot of little things I'd wondered about, why you always seemed to have secrets, why you pulled away." She laughed. "But what are you going to do about everyone who's in love?"

"I don't know." I let go of her hands and started pacing again. "When my powers cause storms, I can stop them if I calm down, but this is different."

Avangeline looked confused, with her eyebrows knit. "Why do you say it like that?"

"Like what?"

"Like you and your powers are separate things?"

"I . . . I don't know." I stopped pacing for a moment. "I guess I've always thought about them that way. I was a normal girl before Samsonville, and then these powers showed up when I moved here. I haven't always had them."

"I mean, maybe not, but they're a part of you now, aren't they?"

I stood there and thought about it. Maybe she was right. Maybe my powers *were* a part of who I was now, even if I hadn't always been this way. I'd started thinking of them as separate because my parents were so scared of what I could do. They loved me. It was the powers that scared them. But maybe trying to separate me from my powers was why things had gotten out of control in the first place. Because when I commanded magic, when I owned my powers, they actually listened to me.

And when I didn't have my powers inside Mrs. Cornwall's house . . . I missed them.

I was a witch.

And despite everything, I liked being this way.

"You're right, Lina," I said. "I'm the same as my powers. I am a witch. And I'm sorry I made you and everyone else fall in love. I hadn't meant to do anything other than get your parents to stay together, but it's my fault."

Suddenly, there was a loud *bang* in the backyard.

Avangeline and I jumped and spun around. The door to the shed—the one that had been stuck shut since we'd first moved in—had blown wide open. And the inside was . . . glowing.

23

We crept toward the shed, Avangeline hiding behind me.

I shielded my eyes, but as I went inside, the golden light faded. There was only one thing in the shed—a pedestal. And on the pedestal was a golden book. I immediately knew: this was a spell book.

I stopped cold. How? How in the world was there a spell book in my aunt's old shed?

"Are you okay, Emmie?" Avangeline asked from outside.

"Sort of," I said.

She peered around the door frame, and her mouth dropped open. "A book? That's beautiful."

She forgot her fear and came closer, leaning down to inspect it.

Unlike Mrs. Cornwall's leather-bound book, this one had a metal cover, but they both had crystals embedded in them. So maybe my mom had been right this whole time: maybe crystals did have powers. Dad and I owed her an apology about her little rock collection.

"It's a spell book," I said. "But I don't understand what it's doing in Aunt Catherine's shed."

"Can you . . . can you open it?" Lina asked.

It hadn't occurred to me that I couldn't. Now, fearing the book rejecting me, I took a small step, ready to be blasted out of the shed. I held out my arm so that Lina stayed back a bit, then braced myself.

When I touched the book, a warm, welcoming feeling spread up my arm and into my chest. Like happy little tingles. I opened the cover, and tucked inside was a piece of paper.

FROM THE DESK OF

CATHERINE DAVIDSON

Dear Emma,

If you found this book, you already know our secret. You've embraced your powers and taken the heavy responsibility that comes with them. You broke the spell I placed on the shed, and for that I'm very proud—breaking a dead woman's spell is no small feat.

I am sorry I was not able to stay in this world to guide you. I sensed your affinity when you were just a baby, and I tried to wait for you to step into your powers, but the truth is some witches never do, and I couldn't hold on any longer. I magicked the house and my pets to look after you, but I'm sorry I had to leave you on your own. I wanted to tell you about our powers, but I felt it was more important for you to have a normal life if you could. I'm still not sure if it was the right decision, but how often do we ever know if what we're doing is truly right? Instead, we do our best.

This is our family's spell book. It contains our knowledge, passed down through generations. Protect it and keep it hidden at all costs.

There is dark magic and there is light. You are the light, Emma—the strongest in generations. Remember that light conquers the dark, but light can also burn.

Catherine

"What does it say?" Avangeline asked.

A lot. It said *a lot*.

"I . . ." I rubbed my temples and handed her the note. Avangeline read it with her lips moving slightly, the way she always did, while I tried to understand everything the note had said.

Emma's Thoughts on the Letter:

1. My great-aunt was a witch
2. She'd placed a spell on the shed and the house and Oliver and Persimmon, which explained a lot
3. She'd left me our family's spell book
4. My great-aunt was a frigging *witch*

Once Lina was done reading, the paper disintegrated, crumbling to ash in her hands.

"No! Did I do that?" Avangeline said, looking horrified.

"I don't think so. I think it just . . . self-destructed." Somewhere inside me, I knew it wasn't her fault. "The paper probably was magicked to turn to dust after it was read twice or something."

"Okay, wow." She stared at her empty hands. "So your aunt was a . . . witch."

"Yeah."

"You didn't know, did you?" she said.

I shook my head, trying not to feel sad or angry that she hadn't told me. But what kind of woman would leave a kid to face this alone? If she'd told me, I could've learned from her. Maybe my powers wouldn't have gone out of control. Maybe I wouldn't have felt so strange this whole time.

"What did she mean about dark magic?" Avangeline asked.

"I'm not sure."

Avangeline's expression turned thoughtful. "Maybe there will be answers in the book."

"Maybe," I said with a small smile.

The truth was I could keep being upset about the life I didn't get, or be happy that I now had all of my family's knowledge in their book. I also had a best friend who loved and accepted me, a house that protected me, and animals to look after me.

Oh, I was going to have words with that cat.

"Come inside with me?" I said.

"Okay," Avangeline said.

I took a step to leave but then remembered the book. I needed to hide it. I gestured like Mrs. Cornwall had, turning my hand in the air, and the book disappeared.

"What the—wow." Avangeline jumped back a few inches and looked all around.

Ugh. She was probably not ready for the truth about Oliver and Persimmon, but I had things to ask them, and she might as well know everything now.

"There's . . . something else you need to know."

"All right." She was still looking at where the book had been as we left the shed.

"Okay, so, um, yeah, I'll just say it: you know how the note said that Oliver and Persimmon were magicked?"

"Yeah . . ."

"Well, they can talk. Like people. Well, Oliver talks just like a person. Persimmon kind of reads minds." I closed my mouth and waited for questions.

Avangeline blinked hard and stayed quiet for a second.

"Okay," she finally said.

We went up to the house. I stopped in front of the door and spread my hands. I slid the bolt in my mind, and it actually worked—the door unlocked.

"Seriously? 'Okay,' that's it?"

She shrugged and sighed. "It kind of is what it is at this point, right?"

I nodded and opened the door to the shop. As soon as I did, the animals rushed up to me.

"Okay, first of all, it was super rude to lock us in," Persimmon said.

"Emma, are you okay?" Oliver said.

Then they noticed Avangeline behind me. They both went completely still and quiet.

"It's okay, guys. She knows."

The three of them all looked at each other. Even though I'd just told Avangeline about Oliver and Persimmon, I knew for a fact that talking animals were a lot to take in. So I understood why she stood there like a statue.

"Emma, what happened? We felt the house tremor," Oliver said.

"I . . . broke the spell," I said.

"You did?" Oliver said, standing straighter.

"The shed opened and . . ." I lifted my hand in the air and turned it. The golden spell book appeared in my hands. Because I wanted it to.

Persimmon looked stunned. So did Oliver. Avangeline started looking a little pale.

"Are you okay?" I asked. The book tried to pull away from me to go hide again. Apparently, spell books also had personalities, like houses and cats. I jumped in the air and caught it.

Lina nodded a couple of times. "It's just . . . it's a lot."

I pursed my lips. It was.

"We couldn't tell you about any of this, Emma," Oliver said. "The house, the shed, the book. Anything."

"Catherine bound us until you did it all on your own," Persimmon said. "It was intensely frustrating."

I frowned, disappointment pulling the corner of my mouth. "Why, though? Just so I could have a shot at being normal? You guys knew from the day after I got here that I had powers. I was never going to be normal."

"But you hadn't accepted your powers or the responsibility that came with them," Oliver said. "And a book that exceptional needs to be in the hands of someone who has done both."

All right, that did make a little bit of sense. I got why no one wanted me to have even more power when I was struggling with what I had naturally. But still, I wished they could've told me.

"It was done to protect you, Emma," Persimmon said. "And everyone else."

I nodded, putting my arms around the book. It nuzzled against me. "So you'll be nicer to me now that I've broken the spell, right?"

The cat raised her nose. "Probably not, no. You're still intensely frustrating."

Well, it was worth a shot.

Avangeline smiled, then rubbed her arms.

"Why is it always so cold in the house?" I asked.

"Magic," Oliver said. "There's so much pooling here because of you that it drops the air temperature."

That made sense . . . in the way anything made sense with magic. But, wait, what was that paragraph about, with the light and the dark?

"Aunt Catherine said there's dark and light magic. And that I'm the light. What does that mean?" I asked. "There are two different kinds?"

Oliver shook his head. "Magic is called dark and light, but all magic is fundamentally the same. The difference is a dark witch will use magic to help herself, while a light witch will use it to help others. Just as people can change, so can witches. A light witch can become dark and vice versa. Obviously, there can also be overlap. You wanted to use your magic to make Avangeline stay for you, but also for her. Because you felt it would ultimately be the best for her."

"You did all of this because you thought it would be best for me?" Avangeline said.

"I'm sorry, again," I said. "I just . . . I wanted to help."

She scratched her head but remained quiet, so I turned back to Oliver and Persimmon.

"Aunt Catherine also said I'm the strongest in generations. What does that mean?" I asked.

"Where did she lose you?" Persimmon said.

So, no, in fact, Persimmon would not be nicer to me now.

"You conjure without words," Oliver said. "All other witches have to use incantations, spells, potions, but you don't have to because there's magic inside you. Not just around you."

I had been right. The power *was* coming from inside me.

"Why?" I asked. "Why am I so powerful?"

"No one knows," Oliver said. "Every five hundred years or so, someone is born this way. It's a confluence of events."

I . . . did not know what that meant.

Persimmon sighed. "All you need to know is you just happened to be this way. Both annoying and extremely powerful."

I would've argued about the annoying part. But what I had to say next wouldn't exactly help my case.

"I think I . . . It's a long story, but I might've accidentally made the whole town fall in love," I said. "Well . . . nine people." I pointed to Avangeline.

Persimmon rolled her eyes so hard she physically turned from me.

"Emma," Avangeline said. "You didn't make me fall in love."

"Yes, I did," I said. "And I'm so sorry. I never meant to."

She shook her head. "I don't feel any different from how I normally do."

Of course she would think that. The spell worked too well.

For just a split second, I thought: *Maybe I should keep her this way.* She'd feel the same incredible thing for me that I felt for her. We'd be together. We'd be happy.

Then Persimmon cleared her throat and stared, unamused by my thoughts.

She was right. I couldn't keep Avangeline this way. It would be wrong. It wouldn't be real. I didn't want Avangeline to love me because I'd forced her to. I wanted her to be able to make the choice for herself. Even if it meant she never wanted anything to do with me.

I let the book float in front of me. "How do I reverse a spell?"

The book shimmied. Apparently it liked when I

asked it questions. Then it turned to an illustrated page of a woman with scissors cutting a golden thread.

To reverse a spell: Find the bindings in your mind.
Pull and shear the magic surrounding the person.
You MUST scatter the binds to prevent reattachment.

"What does this even mean?" I asked. Oliver flew over and looked at it.

"Any time you cast a spell on someone, the person becomes physically wrapped in magic. The binds are what force them to do or think things. You should be able to see the binds and then break them."

I looked at Avangeline, but I didn't see anything. I reached out in my mind, but I didn't feel anything either. She just seemed like Avangeline.

"I don't understand," I said. "Why can't I see anything on her?"

"Because there's no magic surrounding her," Persimmon said. "Open your eyes and ears; she already said she didn't feel any different. People under spells know they feel different—they just don't know why."

I looked from the cat to Avangeline, who smiled and shrugged. But that didn't make sense. I'd accidentally magicked her.

I stared back at the book. "What do you know about love spells?"

The book rapidly flipped pages. It stopped on an

entry about how to make people fall in love. There was a spell, a potion, and a talisman. The text went on for several pages, but there was an asterisk next to the title.

**Hearts that are claimed cannot be changed*

Great. What on earth did that mean?

"It's like everything is written in gibberish," I said. "What does that mean? 'Hearts that are claimed cannot be changed'?"

"It means you need to pay more attention in English class, is what it means," Persimmon said.

I threw my head back and groaned. Honestly. She was the worst cat in the universe.

"It means that it didn't have any effect on Avangeline because her heart already belonged to someone," Oliver said. "Real love is stronger than magic."

I faced Avangeline, and she shrugged.

"I already told you I loved you." She smiled her lopsided grin.

My heart sped up, and I was certain that I was making weird faces as emotions flashed through me. Plus Persimmon said, "You're making weird faces, Emma."

But Avangeline loved me? Really loved me? Not the spell, not a fluke? A warmth flooded my chest, and I was definitely blushing. My mouth felt dry and my palms felt itchy. But what kind of love were we talking about? Did she really feel the same as me? Did she *like* like me?

"Like . . . um, in a . . . crush way?" I said. I somehow avoided cringing at myself, but Persimmon did it for me. Full-body cringed, bringing her shoulders up to her ears.

Lina breathed out a laugh. "Yeah."

And then it hit me: I might be the one who would investigate noises in the dark, but Avangeline was braver than I ever gave her credit for.

"I . . . I feel the same," I said. "I realized it on New Year's Eve. Our hands met, and it just felt like . . . home." I took a deep breath. "I love you, Lina."

I reached out and took her hand. I smiled, and she smiled back, and it was better than magic.

"Well, this is awkward," Persimmon said.

I closed my eyes and sighed loudly.

Avangeline laughed. "I like that they can talk."

"That makes one of us," I said.

"This is all very cute, but don't you have a town to fix?" Persimmon said.

Oh God. With all this, I'd actually managed to forget. I needed to make everything right before my parents got home. And I had . . . not that much time.

"I need to go," I said.

"I'll come with you," Avangeline said. "Maybe I can help."

I nodded. Joy flowed through me. And this time, I let myself feel it. I let happiness flow all the way through me, but nothing happened. No light bulbs burst and no rosebushes bloomed. For the first time, I was really, truly in control of my magic.

I threw my hand up to make the spell book disappear. It accidentally hit the ceiling before I managed to hide it. I grimaced. I swore it was annoyed at me before it vanished, but I was used to things in my house not liking me.

With the book hidden, we grabbed our bikes and rode back into town.

— 24 —

We raced back across Holy Cross Bridge, exchanging smiles. Avangeline loved me and I loved her and it was real. Now we just had to deal with the people who weren't actually in love. The ones who only felt it because of me . . . and the cake.

I couldn't even think about the cake when I was around Persimmon—that's how strong my promise was. When Aunt Catherine's spell book was flipping pages, I'd noticed a page that said an oath between witches was unbreakable. I could never tell anyone about Mrs. Cornwall's powers until she released me from my promise.

Something in the back of my mind said that an adult shouldn't swear me to secrecy like that. I couldn't shake the idea that Mrs. Cornwall might've made everyone fall in love on purpose, but I couldn't figure out why. Probably because it didn't make sense. She wanted me to be her apprentice. She was trying to help me and share her knowledge. I was the one who'd made the spell go out of control by giving the cake to everyone.

No, I just didn't want to take responsibility for what I'd done. It was my magical mess to clean up. My fault.

We got back to Bryan Park, and I scanned the green lawn and colorful blankets. No sign of Mrs. Cornwall, but luckily, all four couples were still there.

Unluckily, they were causing chaos.

Mr. and Mrs. Miles were kissing on their picnic blanket so enthusiastically that several people around them had stopped to stare. In the distance, Old Mr. Day had his fists up to try to fight Mr. Hollis. I wasn't sure why, since they were friends, but I bet it had something to do with Mrs. Antonio, who was trying to break up the fight between the two seventy-year-old men. And worst of all, Mr. Haywood and Miss Sophia had jumped into the Keeble fully dressed and were laughing hysterically as they swam around.

I needed to fix everything, immediately.

Mr. and Mrs. Miles were closest. I stared at them from the edge of the park.

"Do you see the bindings?" Avangeline whispered.

"No."

"Let's get closer," she said.

She took my hand, and it was hard to focus on

anything other than the feel of her fingers in mine. That was, until Mr. and Mrs. Miles started dancing up on each other. Like, grinding-in-a-music-video kind of dancing. Someone was shielding their kindergartener's eyes.

We snuck up until we were only a few feet behind them. I looked them over, but I wasn't sure what a binding would look like . . . until I saw it. It was slight. Just a single golden thread going from her heart to his and back again in a loop.

That was it—the binding.

Now I just had to pull and shear it . . . somehow.

I grabbed ahold of the thread with my magic. The second I connected with it, it fought against me. I arched my back to maintain my hold. But now what? The book had made it seem like a blade should be used to cut the bindings, but it wasn't like I could chase them around with safety scissors. Then I remembered how powerful my magic was. I was the light—the strongest in generations. I commanded it: *Break*.

The binds broke into a million pieces. I pumped my fist, but then the pieces immediately started to reattach. Right, the last step was I had to scatter them. I moved my hands, hoping to push the magic away. It worked!

Mr. and Mrs. Miles suddenly stopped dancing. They stared at each other, looking confused. Then they looked over at me and Lina. We were, like, inches away from them. Even though she couldn't see the binds,

Lina started moving her hands like me. Like we were doing a dance move we'd seen in a viral video or something. We added some jumps and leg kicks too.

Mr. and Mrs. Miles both sat down.

"Shouldn't you kids be somewhere else?" Mrs. Miles snarked. But her heart wasn't in it.

"Yeah," I said. "Sorry."

Lina and I walked away.

"You did it!" Avangeline whispered, squeezing my shoulder.

Old Mr. Day and Mrs. Antonio were next. She had a hand on his chest, trying to keep him away from Mr. Hollis.

"You're making eyes at my woman?" Old Mr. Day yelled. "I'll punch you into next week."

I broke their bonds, and Old Mr. Day put his fists down, although Mr. Hollis kept his up.

"Are you going to take a swing, old man, or not?" Mr. Hollis asked.

"Of course not," Old Mr. Day said. He looked around, bewildered. Then he picked his fedora up off the lawn and put it back on his head.

Mr. Hollis rubbed his KFC beard. "But you said . . ."

"We're old men, Jack," Mr. Day said. "Our fighting days are long over. I'm sorry, Rose, I just . . . I must've gotten carried away."

"Me too," she said, blushing.

Mr. Haywood and Miss Sophia were next after that.

Once I scattered their binds, they immediately got out of the river, looking embarrassed. They stared awkwardly at each other for a moment. Then Mr. Haywood cleared his throat, and Miss Sophia bent to pick up her book from the grass where she'd dropped it.

"Well, I should get back to . . . this," she said, pointing to her novel.

"Right, right. Of course. I should . . . It's time for my walk, anyhow," Mr. Haywood said. He wandered away, but he kept looking back at her.

Everyone looked dazed and awkward after I dispersed their magic. But no one seemed suspicious—just confused. It had worked! Everyone who'd accidentally been enchanted was back to normal without knowing the truth. We'd fixed everything.

"That worked!" I whispered.

"Just my parents left," Avangeline said, looking toward them.

Oh.

"Lina . . ." I stopped on the lawn.

She turned to me and stared with her head tilted.

"Are you sure you want to do this?" I asked. "Look at how happy they are."

Dr. and Mr. Monroe were sitting side by side on their picnic blanket, leaning against each other, with their faces glowing. Max was jumping in little circles around them, looking thrilled. Avangeline and I stared at her family from a few feet away, watching as Mr. Monroe leaned down and kissed Dr. Monroe's forehead.

"If I leave them this way, they'll stay together and you'll stay here," I said. "Don't you want that?"

Avangeline sighed. "I do, more than anything, but it wouldn't be real."

"It *is* real, Lina. This is really what they're feeling. They'll be happy—you all will."

Avangeline shook her head, looking sad. "You know, they used to look at each other like that when I was younger. But . . . seeing them now makes me realize they haven't been this way in years. The divorce seemed like it was out of nowhere, but . . . it wasn't. They haven't been in love in a while. And they tried to tell me, but I couldn't understand."

I gripped her hand. "But if I undo it . . . you'll leave. You won't have your family anymore. You won't have me anymore."

My eyes stung and I sighed. Before I could stop it, a tear escaped, rolling down my cheek. Avangeline reached out and wiped it away. The pad of her thumb traced over my skin.

She smiled slightly, even though her eyes were glassy. "I'll always have a family, Emmie—the same way we'll always have each other. It'll just be different, that's all. But it's not right to make people stay together. Not when the love is gone."

She was right and I knew it, but that didn't make it any easier. Darkness was easier. I started to understand what Oliver meant about how a light witch could turn dark. I knew that if I gave in to this feeling, I could always find a reason to give in. To use magic to get what I wanted. But forcing other people to do what I wanted them to do was wrong.

No. I had to be the light, even if it burned.

Ugh. That note. Now I got what Aunt Catherine was saying, and this was the worst.

Before I could think any more about it, I pulled the bindings off Avangeline's parents. I moved my hands and scattered all the magic remaining. I nodded at Lina that it was done.

"You're the bravest person I know, Emmie." She squeezed my hand, and we walked up to her family's blanket.

"No," I said. "You are."

Dr. Monroe had been sitting on Mr. Monroe's lap, but as soon as I broke their bond, she moved away with a confused look on her face. Mr. Monroe looked just as puzzled by what he'd been doing. He cleared his throat, and she rubbed the back of her neck as they avoided looking at each other.

"Where did you disappear to, Avangeline?" Dr. Monroe asked.

"I helped Emmie carry some of the bake sale stuff,"

she said. "Do you mind if we go to her house for a while?"

"Oh, um, sure, kiddo," Mr. Monroe said. He still had that dazed look the other couples had. Like he couldn't figure out what had changed but knew he didn't feel the same way he just had.

"That's fine, honey," Dr. Monroe said. "Be back by dinner."

Just like that, it was over. The spell was broken, and they were back to normal. Avangeline would still move at the end of July like nothing had happened. I'd gone through all of this for nothing.

I wanted to curl into a ball and cry, but Avangeline took my hand again as we walked away.

"Thank you, Emmie," she said as we approached our bikes.

"I didn't want to do it," I said.

"I know," she said. "But you did because it was the right thing to do."

25

We rode back home, and even though I was a mess with my feelings, somehow I knew I wouldn't call in any storms. I'd accepted who I was and that doing the right thing, being the light, would really, really suck sometimes.

I glanced over at Avangeline, and she smiled that lopsided grin. She loved me. And I loved her. And I was going to miss her with all my heart.

As we pedaled, I couldn't shake the thought that Mrs. Cornwall had wanted all of this to happen. She could've warned me not to give the cake to anyone but Dr. Monroe, but she hadn't.

I thought back to my aunt's note, and then something else stuck out to me. Aunt Catherine had sensed my magic as a baby. Witches could sense each other.

So there was no way Mrs. Cornwall and Aunt Catherine hadn't known about each other.

Mrs. Cornwall knew my aunt practiced magic. *That* was why she'd been convinced I had a spell to grow the peach tree. And why she'd been confused that I didn't know where magic came from. But she'd never said a word to me. Knowledge was power, and she'd kept the secret from me.

She'd known there was a spell book hidden at my house.

And she was hoping to find it.

My cheeks tingled as blood left my face.

"Emmie, are you okay?"

I tried to tell her. After everything that had happened, I didn't want to keep any more secrets from Avangeline, but as soon as I thought about Mrs. Cornwall's powers, I couldn't move my tongue.

It all felt so icky and wrong. And I kicked myself—I'd known all along there was something up with Mrs. Cornwall, and I'd let other people, like my parents, tell me that I was imagining it.

"It's just . . . it's a lot," I said. That was as close to the truth as I could come.

She nodded sympathetically, and then we turned toward my house.

My parents' old Honda was in the driveway, and I pushed my thoughts about Mrs. Cornwall aside. I wouldn't trust her ever again, and that was enough for now. Right now I had to deal with my parents. I wasn't sure if I should tell them about the book and Aunt Catherine and how Avangeline knew everything. I didn't want to, and what was another secret when we had a heap of them?

No. I shook my head. No more secrets—I had to tell them.

But maybe I'd wait for tomorrow. Too much had happened to explain everything today.

I'd just put my kickstand out when I noticed something strange. The doors to the shop were wide open, and we never left them like that.

I ran up the steps, and the house shuddered a warning, the wood of the porch vibrating under my feet. Something was wrong. I felt it in my core. A chill spread over me, like someone dropping an ice cube down my back.

"Mom? Dad?" I yelled. "Mom! Dad!"

No response.

I ran inside, yelling again and again for them and for Oliver and Persimmon, but no one was inside.

"Maybe they're in the backyard," Lina said.

We walked into the kitchen to go outside, and then I saw it.

Taped on the glass of the kitchen door was a note on Collingsworth's Bakery paper, written in perfect script.

The book for your parents

26

Avangeline grabbed the note off the door. "What does this mean? Who wrote this?"

I tried to tell her, but my tongue wouldn't work. Of course it wouldn't. I gestured with my palms up, but I couldn't do more than shrug.

"Seriously, Emmie? Even after everything today, you can't be honest with me?" Avangeline said.

"No. No, that's not it at all. I want to tell you . . . I just can't," I said. Which totally sounded like I didn't want to tell her. I grabbed my hair in frustration. "Please, you have to trust me. You need to get out of here. It's not safe."

I was furious with myself. I'd been so desperate to keep Avangeline from moving that I'd ignored every bad feeling I got from Mrs. Cornwall.

"What do you mean, Emmie?" Avangeline asked, her eyes wide. She reread the note. "Is Mrs. Cornwall . . . bad?"

I opened my mouth to speak but couldn't get anything out. I tried to answer her with my eyes and blinked twice. Avangeline knew me so well. I could see the pieces falling into place for her.

"The spell book," Lina whispered. "She wants the spell book. Oh, Emmie. All the times you tried to tell us there was something off about her. She's a witch, isn't she?"

Again I couldn't answer. But she knew me to my core and could see the truth.

"What are you going to do?" Lina asked.

"Give her the book, I guess," I said. "I don't think I have a choice."

Lina's shoulders slumped. "Emmie, there has to be another way."

There wasn't. I hung my head as tears pooled in my eyes. The book belonged to me, to my family. My aunt had trusted me to protect it, and I'd failed on the first day. The knowledge inside would've helped me control and focus my magic, and I hadn't even gotten to read it yet. And by giving Mrs. Cornwall all that power, I'd be making a dark witch that much stronger. I didn't know what she'd use it for, exactly, but I knew it wouldn't be good.

I hesitated. Maybe Avangeline was right—maybe there was another way and I just hadn't thought of it yet.

All of a sudden, a scream pierced the air. It was coming from inside Mrs. Cornwall's house.

Mom.

My blood curdled and my magic swirled, ready. Sparks lit up in a halo around me. Lina took a step back, eyes wide.

My parents were more important than any book. I'd let Mrs. Cornwall have it to make sure they were safe.

"I need you to go back home," I said to Avangeline.

She shook her head, even though she was trembling.

"It's okay, Lina. I swear it'll be okay. But I don't want her to get you too," I said. "I need you to go. Now."

Honestly, I didn't know if I'd be okay. But I had to make sure Lina was out of harm's way.

"Please?" I said. "I . . . I can't risk you getting hurt."

My voice broke as I asked. I stared into Lina's eyes, and she looked back at me. Then she sighed.

"Okay, Emmie. I'll go," she said.

We held hands and walked to the driveway together.

I waited until she got on her bike and pedaled away. I forced myself to smile as she kept looking back at me until she was out of sight. And then I took a deep breath. I looked at the house, and it groaned a mournful sound. I patted the railing. It wasn't the house's fault.

It was Mrs. Cornwall's.

I went over to her house with harder, braver steps than I felt. At least Avangeline was out of danger. I'd trade the spell book to Mrs. Cornwall and save my parents. It would all be okay.

The door to Mrs. Cornwall's house opened as I approached.

I stepped inside, and there, tied up back-to-back in the living room, were my parents. Floating in a glass orb above them were Persimmon and Oliver.

And then the door slammed shut behind me.

27

The door to the kitchen swung open as the front door closed. Mrs. Cornwall came into the living room looking as neat and proper as usual. She'd changed out of her skirt suit into a T-shirt and capris. There wasn't a wrinkle on her, despite her holding my entire family hostage.

"There you are, little witch," Mrs. Cornwall said with a smile. "We've been waiting for you."

"Emmie, go! Run!" Mom shouted.

"Oh, Ellen, we said we were going to behave." Mrs. Cornwall tsked. "Silence binds the wayward tongue."

She turned her fingers, and a magical bind covered my mom's mouth. Mom's eyes widened as she struggled, and then her shoulders drooped as she realized she couldn't fight it.

"That's more neighborly," Mrs. Cornwall said with a ghost of a smile.

Overhead, Oliver flapped and Persimmon scratched against the glass, but they couldn't break free.

"Slumber until I say wake." Mrs. Cornwall lowered her hands, and both animals suddenly collapsed into a deep sleep.

"Enough," I said.

"If we're finally done with distractions," Mrs. Cornwall said. She looked at my dad, whose head dipped in a reluctant nod.

My parents both looked so frightened, so confused. My heart wrenched, and fury built in me like I'd never felt before. At home it would've caused a raging fire, but in Mrs. Cornwall's living room, nothing happened.

"Only one witch can conjure in a house, my dear," Mrs. Cornwall said, shaking her head. "I would've thought Catherine would've told you *something* important. Instead of leaving a silly little witch to figure everything out on her own."

I tried to talk and couldn't.

Mrs. Cornwall rolled her eyes. "Oh, for the love of . . . I release you from your oath."

My tongue worked again.

"I thought you wanted to work together, for me to be

your apprentice," I said. "Why do this when we said we'd share our knowledge?"

I already knew the answer, but I needed to get her talking and give myself time to think. How was I going to get all of us out safely? In movies and TV shows, villains loved to talk about themselves and their evil plans. Maybe Mrs. Cornwall was the same.

"Oh, Emma." She laughed. "Why would I share my power with a foolish little girl? I just needed you to break Catherine's spell and get her book. I figured that if you really needed it, the book would show itself to you."

"You made everyone fall in love on purpose," I murmured. "You used dark magic."

She rolled her eyes. "Dark magic? I made wretched, miserable people happy—where is the evil in that? And it's not like you weren't willing to do whatever it took to make your crush stay."

I looked to the side. She had me there. It was so easy to use our powers to make people do what we wanted. But it was also wrong.

Mom and Dad stared back and forth between us. I wondered if they were putting together that Aunt Catherine had been a witch and that was why she'd left everything to us.

"But enough of this. You're here because you agree to my exchange," Mrs. Cornwall said, her eyes hungry. "The book, if you please."

She held out her hand.

"Why do you want it?" I asked.

"Why do I want to have the Davidsons' line of power so that I could enchant the whole town rather than just baked goods?" Mrs. Cornwall said. "I can't imagine."

Oh God. She wanted the whole town under her control.

Think, Emma. Think.

"Cast my family out of this house and back into mine, and I will give you the spell book," I said.

I finally had a plan . . . or, well, something like a plan, at least. With my family safe, maybe I could conjure a fake spell book.

But Mrs. Cornwall's sharp eyes were on me.

"No tricks, little witch," Mrs. Cornwall said. "Swear it."

Darn. "I swear," I said. I felt another oath swirl around me.

Okay, so there went my one and only plan. Now that I was bound, I couldn't loophole my way out.

"It's always the ones who deserve power the least who are given the most." Mrs. Cornwall laughed. I didn't even have time to think about what she said, because she looked at my parents and pets. "Out. Return home. Never to step foot across my threshold again."

She waved her hand, and the door opened. My parents, Oliver, and Persimmon flew out of the house, floating on air. I watched as they were carried back into my home. Our shop doors closed behind them—they were safe.

"You didn't bind them from talking about this," I said.

"I don't need to. They can't expose me without the risk of exposing you."

I bit my lip. She was right, but why didn't she enchant them anyway, just to be safe? It seemed odd.

"Now, the book, Emma," she said.

"I can't conjure in your house," I said. "And I don't have it on me." I gestured to my T-shirt and shorts.

Mrs. Cornwall sighed. "Outside, then."

We stepped onto the porch and then down the stairs, until we were right in front of her house. I wasn't sure if enchantments covered porches, but I suspected they did.

I took a deep breath. I was out of options. I had no choice but to give her the real spell book. To lose all my family's secrets and power. Sadness filled my chest, bringing me down like an anchor. I'd only just proven myself worthy of the book, and now it was being yanked away. By someone who'd use it against the whole town.

She was right about me: I was a naive little girl. I hadn't listened to my own gut about her. I'd let everyone else tell me that what I knew wasn't true. And now I'd lost everything. Well . . . almost everything. She couldn't take my magic. And I silently swore I'd fight her. Somehow.

I slowly reached into the air and pulled out the book. Warmth filled my hand, like the book was saying a familiar hello. Mrs. Cornwall's eyes grew big. The gold of the cover shimmered in my hands, and I clung to it. Every ounce of me didn't want her to have Aunt Catherine's book. But a deal was a deal. My family was safe, and that was what was most important.

I extended it to her.

Mrs. Cornwall had just put her fingertips on the cover when Avangeline jumped out of a bush and tore the book from her grasp.

28

Once Avangeline had the book, she broke into a run.

Mrs. Cornwall raised her hands to conjure.

"No!" I screamed.

Avangeline paused and looked at me, my scream getting her to stop instead of run. I called a gust of wind and blasted Mrs. Cornwall back until she was knocked down onto her perfect lawn. The wind chimes on her porch made a horrible sound, screeching rather than chiming.

"Run, Lina! Get inside the house!" I yelled. "It'll protect you." But in the second I turned my head, Mrs. Cornwall was on her feet again.

"Fire, alight around the girl," Mrs. Cornwall said. A circle of tall flames lit up around Avangeline, stopping her in her tracks.

No!

I gathered a breath and exhaled, wanting to put the fire out. Suddenly, the flame disappeared. Like I blew out a candle rather than a circle of flames. I stared at Mrs. Cornwall. She could've hurt Lina. I focused all my anger, feeling it burn inside me, and then I let it go. A wall of fire ten feet high lit up in front of Mrs. Cornwall.

The fire was so hot I took a step back.

"Ice, cool the hottest tempers and free me," she said. The fire went out, and she stepped through the smoke.

I stared, dismayed. It was so easy for her to counter my magic. The thing that had taken me so long to control. The thing I still couldn't entirely handle.

And right then I thought: *I can't win.* How could I beat someone who had thirty years of practice?

"Daggers form and daggers fly," Mrs. Cornwall said, lifting her arm.

A horrific snapping sound filled the air as branches broke off the trees and sharpened into a thousand wooden daggers. I gasped. How was that even possible? But I didn't have time to wonder because they were heading straight for Avangeline. How was I going to stop them all? A shield? Turning them around? What if I missed one? What if Avangeline . . . No, I couldn't even think about losing her. I didn't understand spells like Mrs. Cornwall. But I had to try.

I waved my hands in the air, frantic, with one thought: protect Avangeline.

Suddenly, the daggers changed into pink carnations—Lina's favorite flower. Gently, they floated down onto the lawn. I watched them, amazed that my magic knew what to do. Avangeline stopped and looked over her shoulder at me. She almost smiled at the drizzle of carnations, but then kept running. She trusted me to have her back. And I would protect her. At all costs.

"You're strong, little witch," Mrs. Cornwall said with a sneer. "But I have age and experience. You won't win."

I gulped, standing with my feet apart and my hands ready. My breath came fast, my body swaying as I tried to predict what she'd do next.

Mrs. Cornwall pointed her hands down and said, "Earth, split and swallow her up."

The ground tore like a canyon, a rift heading right for Avangeline.

No. Cushion her. I waved my arm over the ground, and thousands, maybe millions, of feathers filled the cracks as quickly as they formed. Avangeline stumbled, but the feathers caught her.

I didn't know how many more times my powers could save her. But I couldn't keep waiting to see how Mrs. Cornwall would try to hurt Lina next. I needed to stop her. She was the problem. She was trying to trap my friend. My family. Me.

Electricity sizzled in my blood. Lightning was deadly, but she deserved whatever happened to her, right? She was the one who started all this.

I let go.

A bolt of lightning zigzagged out of the blue sky. But as it streaked down, I realized it would kill her and I couldn't do that. I couldn't murder someone. At the last minute, I re-aimed, and the lightning crashed right at Mrs. Cornwall's feet. She looked down, then at me.

"Enough!" I said, my voice booming.

"You can't harm me with light magic, little witch. What is a single candle in the middle of a dark night?" Mrs. Cornwall's lips turned up, even though she was breathing hard. Her voice had a rasp like when Old Mr. Day had pneumonia. But then Mrs. Cornwall ran her hands down in front of herself. "The speed of ages."

She broke into an unnaturally fast run after Avangeline. And I knew I couldn't keep up. Maybe she was right: I couldn't win with light magic.

But there was more than one kind of magic.

Catch her. Stop her.

I circled my arms, and thick vines grew out of the ground, coming from all angles. Wisteria. They caught Mrs. Cornwall, and she yelled as the vines dragged her to the ground. Victory raced through me, thickening the vines to the size of ship ropes. I kept growing them until they encased her. She tried to cast a spell, but the wisteria bound her hands. And then it dawned on me that she needed both her words and her hands to conjure.

Maybe I should've started with her hands to begin

with, but it wasn't like I'd ever been in a witch fight before.

It didn't matter, though. I'd won! My heart hammered against my rib cage, my hands and knees shaky, but I'd done it. I'd stopped Mrs. Cornwall. I'd protected Avangeline.

With Mrs. Cornwall trapped on the ground, I slowly walked over to the tangle of vines. She was wheezing, and blood trickled from the corners of her lips. But she hadn't been injured.

"What is that?" I asked.

She coughed, and more blood came out. I flinched.

"The cost of conjuring. The one you don't feel." She sneered again and stared coldly into my eyes. "You don't deserve your powers."

Anger built inside me. She'd kidnapped my family and tried to hurt Avangeline, all just to get more power, and she didn't feel even a little sorry. Instead, she was just . . . jealous of me.

"Swear to me now you won't come after my family or Avangeline again," I said.

Mrs. Cornwall laughed.

"Swear it." I splayed my hands and sent sharp thorns up through the vines.

Some part of me was happy to use my anger. To punish her. She deserved it for what she'd done. Even if she wasn't a threat right now. Even if she hadn't actually hurt the people I loved—she'd tried to and that was enough.

I grew the thorns inch by inch until she screamed. And then I kept going.

"Emma!" Avangeline shouted. "Stop!"

I looked up. Lina was standing on my porch. She seemed like she was on the verge of tears. I wondered if she was hurt, but she was staring at the tangle of wisteria. Then I looked, really looked, at what I was doing. I was hurting Mrs. Cornwall with my powers. And I wanted to hurt her more, even though Lina and my family were safe, because I was angry. I wanted to eliminate her even though I wasn't in danger.

This was darkness, not light. And it was so tempting.

"Maybe I was wrong about you, little witch," Mrs. Cornwall cackled.

The darkness, the bad part of me, said to send those sharp thorns right through her. To end this.

"Just leave her," Avangeline said. "Come with me."

I still thought about it, but I took a breath. Avangeline was okay. My family was okay.

I walked away.

After a few steps, I raised my hands over my head and set a protection dome over our entire property.

She is never to come here again.

Avangeline looked up at the sky, waiting at the edge of my porch.

I went up the stairs, my legs feeling like Jell-O, until we were face-to-face. The weight of what had happened started to hit me. I hadn't had much time to think in the moment, but Avangeline could've been taken from me for good if I'd been a second slower or a little less powerful.

But she was here. Like dawn after the worst night.

"What are you even doing here? I told you to go," I said.

"You said you needed me to leave. You didn't say anything about me coming back." She reached out and took my hand.

I almost smiled. I'd just been loopholed by Avangeline.

"Here," she said. From behind her back, she pulled out my family's spell book. Not only had she stayed when she knew there was danger, but she'd saved my family's knowledge and the whole town from Mrs. Cornwall.

Energy, magic, and love flowed from my toes up to my shoulders. I stood on the balls of my feet and pressed my lips to her cheek.

I pulled back, scared that was too much, but she was beaming.

But I only had a second to smile before a pair of arms grabbed us from behind.

29

My parents hugged us and looked us over and hugged us again. The ropes Mrs. Cornwall had used were on the shop floor—they'd somehow found a way out of them.

"Oh my God, Emmie," Dad said. Mom was silent, and then I saw the gold thread. I pulled at it with my mind, sheared it, and flung the magic away, fanning her face with my hands.

Mom touched her mouth and let out a big breath. "Oh God, what happened? What in the world?"

My parents looked at each other and then stared at me. Mom arched an eyebrow, and Dad's forehead creased.

"So, um, yeah, some things happened while you were gone," I said.

"Yes, I think we're aware," Dad said. He put his hands

on top of his head and then ran them down his face. "I saw it, and I still don't believe it."

Just then Persimmon and Oliver floated by. I grabbed the orb and set it on the floor. I placed my hand on top, told the glass to dissolve, and it did. My parents watched, astonished. Avangeline just smiled.

I spun the magic off Oliver and Persimmon so they would wake up. They came to suddenly, Oliver still flapping and Persimmon scratching the floor.

"Oh, Emma, what happened?" Oliver said.

Persimmon looked around. "We're back home?"

"They can talk?" Mom asked. "They can talk. Okay. So . . . they can talk?"

She made a horrified noise.

Okay, maybe it hadn't been the *best* idea to keep so many secrets from my parents.

I felt the urge to reach for a lie to smooth it all over, but it was time to come clean. Lying had caused so many problems. Maybe the truth would be better. At least I could try.

I drew a deep breath and told them everything, from how Mrs. Cornwall was a witch to how Aunt Catherine had been a witch, too and the spell she put on the shed. It took a while to explain—longer than with Avangeline, because they kept interrupting to ask questions. And there were some seriously disapproving looks when I got to the part about making people in town fall in love. But finally I was done. I turned my hand, and the spell book floated straight up. It did a pirouette in the air before disappearing.

I wasn't sure if the book was more dramatic or the cat.

"What do we do now, Phil?" Mom asked, her eyes concerned.

Dad pursed his lips.

"About what?" I asked.

"Well, about the fact that Avangeline knows everything, honey," Mom said.

"Hmm, that is a . . . pickle," Dad said.

"Unless . . . maybe Emmie can make her forget . . ." Mom said.

I stared at them and blinked a few times. I couldn't have heard her right. I looked at Avangeline, and she looked down to the side, pursing her lips. But she didn't have to say anything; I'd never erase her mind, even if I could.

"*That's* your biggest concern from everything I just said?" I asked.

"We're just worried about you," she said.

I shook my head. "You care more about keeping my powers a secret than anything else that happened."

"No, of course not, Emmie," Mom said.

I frowned. "It was the first thing you said. Are you that ashamed of me?"

Mom turned pale. "We're not ashamed of you, Emmie. We love you."

"We just want to make sure you're safe," Dad added.

"You're ashamed of my magic, and my magic is part of me. So you are."

My eyes stung, but I refused to cry. I held my head up.

"Emmie, we never wanted you to be ashamed of who you are," Dad said. My mom nodded.

"But how else am I supposed to feel? Lina isn't freaked out by me. Telling her, owning that my powers are a part of me, was what broke the spell, but all you care about is that she knows."

"We love Avangeline, but I just don't think the world is ready to know about you," Mom said. "It's amazing that you have these abilities, but not everyone will think so."

I shook my head. "We're not talking about the world. We're talking about my best friend, who just saved our family's spell book and made sure a ton of power didn't fall into evil hands."

Mom was silent and chewed on her lip.

"I know, honey, but—" Dad began.

"You're right, Emma," Mom said. Dad stopped and turned toward her. "We've been loving you despite your magic, but it is a part of you. And you were right about Mrs. Cornwall this whole time, and we were the ones who tried to convince you she was okay."

"I did too," Avangeline said quietly.

"You're right about Avangeline too," Mom said. "Thank you, Lina, for everything you've done to help Emmie."

Lina blushed and shrugged.

I took a breath. I had one more thing to say. One I wasn't sure they'd agree with, but keeping the secret of who I was had caused so many problems.

"I think I should decide who to tell about my powers and when," I said.

My parents exchanged glances.

"I don't know, Emma . . ." Dad said.

"We're scared for you," Mom said. "We accept you, and Lina does too, but not everyone will."

"But shouldn't I get to decide who I trust instead of hiding forever? It hasn't been . . . great. It's made me a liar, and lying is wrong. I just feel wrong all the time."

"Oh, Emma," Mom said. "We never wanted you to feel that way—to feel like you're wrong. We did what we thought was best, but maybe we were the ones who were wrong."

Dad took a breath and then nodded. "You're right. Asking you to pretend to be normal and stay hidden didn't work. We're sorry, Emma. It's terrifying, honestly, but from now on, you tell the people you trust."

"And if you make a mistake, I'm sure your spell book can help," Avangeline added.

I hadn't thought about that—trusting someone I shouldn't. I'd known deep down that Mrs. Cornwall was bad, but what if I misjudged someone I thought was good? That was a new kind of scary, but Lina was right: I had my family's knowledge and history to help me. Along with two parents who supported me. A magical bird who was there for me. A best friend who loved me. And . . . Persimmon.

We all hugged again, and tears fell down my cheeks. They were happy, sad, and exhausted tears. But everyone I loved was safe and loved me too.

"What do we do about Mrs. Cornwall?" I asked. "I cast a protection dome over our property, but with her next door . . . how can we ever really be safe? She wants the book, and I'm sure she won't just stop now."

My parents exchanged glances.

"I'm not sure, Emmie," Mom said.

Dad glanced out the shop window. "We can come up with a plan, but for now you should free her."

"Really?" I asked. "But—"

"We can't just leave her out there like that," Dad said. He didn't look happy about releasing her either, though.

"No, someone might see," Mom said.

She had a point. Someone could drive by and see a mess of unnatural vines, carnations, and feathers, and then what? We were lucky that with all of the town at the picnic, no one had driven down the road and witnessed the magical fight.

We all stepped outside.

"Stay right here," Mom said.

"But there's a protection . . . Okay, Mom," I said. We'd all been through a lot, and I could undo the magical vines right from the porch. No need to freak her out by going too close.

I moved my fingers, directing the vines to unravel slowly, erasing them from the roots up. I didn't need to use my hands, but I had more control when I did. I stood ready to encase Mrs. Cornwall in glass if she tried to strike at me or anyone I loved. But as the vines vanished, there was . . . nothing.

Mrs. Cornwall was gone.

I scanned her yard, looking for her, but she'd just . . . disappeared.

"What the heck?" I said.

"I . . . I don't know," Dad said.

My parents, Avangeline, and I all walked down the steps and over to the property line. I reached out to try to feel her magic, to see if she was hiding somewhere, but there was . . . nothing.

She'd vanished into thin air.

"She's gone," I said. "She was tied up right in there." I pointed to where the vines had been.

"That's . . ." Mom cleared her throat and started to look pale. "It's impossible, but I guess nothing really is."

The only signs there'd been a fight were scorch marks from the lightning and fire, and wide swaths of feathers and carnations. I covered all of it with green grass, and it was like nothing had happened at all.

I was certain we hadn't seen the last of Mrs. Cornwall. She might come back for the book or to get revenge one day, and I'd have to be ready for her, but for now we were safe.

We were still looking at the ground where Mrs. Cornwall had been when Dr. Monroe's car pulled up into our driveway. She put it in park and got out.

"Avangeline, I was worried," she said, sounding breathless.

"Hi, Mom," Lina said. Her eyes were wide, but she kept her voice steady.

I could feel Mom and Dad tense up. Had Dr. M. seen something? Had she heard something?

"Ava, I texted and you didn't answer—we've talked about that," Dr. Monroe said. "I thought maybe you got hit by a car or were kidnapped!"

Avangeline blew out a breath. "Oh, I'm sorry, Mom. I forgot, and then Emmie's parents came home and we were talking to them and I forgot again."

"Oh, hi, Ellen. Phil," Dr. Monroe said.

My parents threw on smiles and exchanged pleasantries with Lina's mom as Avangeline snuck a little thumbs-up at me. Her mom didn't suspect anything.

Then Dr. M. turned to Avangeline. "It's time to come home."

"I'd like to stay," Avangeline said quietly.

Dr. Monroe hesitated. "I suppose you could stay another half hour, but Ava—"

"That's not what I mean," Avangeline said. She stood up straighter and put her shoulders back. "I want to stay here, in Samsonville. Whenever I'm not in school. I understand that you and Dad don't want to be together anymore, but it's not fair to make me leave my father and my friends. I'm *not* okay with that. And you know I hate the nickname Ava."

Dr. Monroe stood still and blinked a couple of times. I was pretty stunned too.

"Lina . . ." her mom began.

"I know you both think I'm too young to decide, but I'm twelve and a half. I have a life here. I don't want to leave Samsonville forever. It breaks my heart."

Dr. Monroe opened and closed her mouth several times. "You've never said anything like this."

"I have, but you don't hear me. You talk over me and treat me like I'm the same age as Max."

"Oh, honey," Dr. Monroe said. "I'm sorry. I just . . . you're my baby."

"But I'm not a baby anymore."

Dr. M. frowned. "I know. It's hard for me sometimes."

Lina looked down at the ground. "I'm sorry, Mom."

Dr. Monroe sighed. "You shouldn't be. You're turning into a young woman—one I'm very proud of."

Avangeline's chin shook, and Dr. M. opened her arms. Avangeline rushed to her mother and hugged her.

"I'll . . . *we* will talk to your father," Dr. M. said. "I didn't mean to make you totally leave him and Samsonville behind. I just thought it would be easier for you to have a clean break. But maybe I was thinking about myself." She paused and sighed. "I'm sorry, Avangeline. I'm sure we can arrange something for summers and holidays—something where you split the time between here and New Orleans for as long as you want."

"I'd really like that, Mom," Lina said.

Splitting time? Hope bubbled inside me and then overflowed, and the sun shone brighter. Lina wouldn't be gone for good. Now that she'd stood up to her mother, she'd be back every break. I wouldn't go more than a few months without seeing her. It was more than I'd hoped for, and all because Avangeline was so brave.

"Anything we can do to help, you know we're here, and we always love to have Avangeline with us," Dad said.

I smiled at my parents. Dad's arm was wrapped around Mom's shoulders, and she leaned into him.

"Thank you both," Dr. Monroe said. "Avangeline, are you coming with me?"

Lina nodded. "In just a second."

Dr. M. got into her car, and Avangeline gave me a hug. I hugged her back.

"Thank you," I said. "You're the best friend in the world and the bravest girl I know."

"That's what I was going to say." Avangeline's eyes had tears in them, but she smiled.

"So you'll be back . . ." I said.

She smiled. "Every chance I get."

"I still wish you weren't going," I said.

Lina sighed. "I know. Things are going to change, but we'll be the same."

"I'll see you soon," I said.

"Yes, you will."

She smiled her lopsided grin and then got into the passenger seat. My parents and I waved until the car disappeared. And then we went back inside the house together.

— Epilogue —

Two Months Later

I won't lie: it was really hard to say goodbye to Avangeline. But at least I got to spend my thirteenth birthday with her. My new beehive was keeping me busy, and so were my . . . lessons. But, still, I missed her a lot. I was counting down the days until she came home for Halloween.

"Em," Dad said.

I'd been caught staring off again. Dad had taken it upon himself to become my full-time magic tutor, with the help of Aunt Catherine's spell book.

"Really focus now," Dad said.

He threw a softball at me, and I turned it to bubbles with a flick of my wrist. A rock came hurtling at me right after, and I shattered it into pebbles. Then a wrench came spiraling at me. It nearly hit me, because who tosses a wrench at their beloved only child? I turned the metal into a full-size garden bench.

"You were late on the wrench," he said, folding his arms.

"You almost killed me!" I said.

"You need to be prepared for anything, Em," he said.

It was the weirdest summer school ever.

"How's it going out here?" Mom came out onto the back porch. "Oh, what a beautiful bench. I like the details, Emmie."

I gestured with my hand, like: *Ta-da!*

"Do you mind if we—" Mom asked.

"It'll look great in the store," I said.

They'd closed Occult & Davidson and turned it into Davidson's Flower Shop, a real store for the floral business, and it was doing very well. I made vases and one-of-a-kind benches for them to sell, along with continuing to grow whatever came to mind in our garden. My parents believed my magic just *happened* to make a lot of garden-related things for the store. So, yes, I still had some secrets from them, but very small ones.

"He almost hit her with a wrench," Persimmon said.

Dad and I both side-eyed her. The cat was out on the grass pouncing on butterflies, but she hadn't killed anything. That was our deal: she could go outside, but no murder. She didn't like it but said it was better than being *"cooped up with a know-it-all bird who reads all the time."*

Oliver had gotten into novels and enjoyed talking about them at length with Dad. Like the world's strangest book club.

Persimmon walked up to Mom and circled her ankles. Mom smiled, then frowned at us. She'd started taking allergy meds so she could pet Persimmon.

"Did you really, Phil?" Mom asked.

"She has to be prepared for the unexpected," Dad said.

Mom sighed. "Well, I think it's probably enough practice for today. What do you say we get ice cream?"

Dad and I exchanged glances and then sprinted toward the car.

"Speed of ages," I said. I ran inhumanly fast across the lawn and dove into the back seat of the Honda.

"No fair," Dad said, getting into the driver's seat.

I put my palms up.

Mom smiled at us as she got in, and we drove over to Morrisey's ice cream stand. Since it was a late-summer night, it was the most crowded place in Samsonville. Old Mr. Day and Mrs. Antonio were sitting side by side on the porch swing, welcoming the crowd. They'd started dating after the disaster in Bryan Park. Turned out they'd been in love when they were teenagers and had been reminiscing during Founder's Day. I'm not sure how much the love spell had to do with it, but I was glad they were happy.

No one was sure what had happened to Mrs. Cornwall. The day after she vanished, a note had been found on the bakery that said Closed Until Further Notice. It was written in her perfect script, and I got a chill any time I thought about it.

But the only chill I cared about that night was Morrisey's ice cream. We got in line, and I looked at the day's options for soft serve. Tonight it was pistachio or mocha.

"What'll it be, Em?" Dad asked.

"Definitely mocha. Large cone, please."

"You'll get more dripped onto you than in your mouth," Mom said.

I had a freezing spell, but I couldn't use it. I'd agreed not to use magic in public, so I frowned and said, "All right, a medium . . . with chocolate dip."

Mom sighed but tousled my hair.

"Emma?" a voice asked.

I turned. It was Isabella. She already had her ice cream cone and was almost done. Of course she hadn't dripped at all. Her parents were by their car, arguing. So not much had changed there.

"Hey," I said. "How's it going?"

"I just got back from visiting family," she said.

"Oh, that's right," I said. She'd texted me from Massachusetts. "How was Salem?"

After Avangeline had left, Isabella and I were sitting by ourselves on opposite sides of the Keeble one day, and we started talking. I apologized for lying to her years ago about her birthday party. We both showed up the next day at the same time and talked to each other from across the water again. Then the day after that, we sat on the same side.

"It was fun but long—especially the drive with *them*." She laughed. "It's good to be back. I was thinking about hopping over to the library tomorrow to check out the new books. Want to come with?"

"Sure." I'd given Miss Sophia all the money from the bake sale the day after the picnic, and she was so happy she cried. Weirdly enough, even though I was certain there was no magic left on them, she and Mr. Haywood were also dating now and more in love than I'd ever seen two people.

"Great, I'll text you." Isabella waved goodbye and walked away with her parents.

My parents gave me a thumbs-up, happy I'd made another friend.

"Losers," I said, laughing.

After the ice cream, we raced home so I could get in front of my laptop by nine o'clock. It was Friday, and Friday was the best day because that's when Avangeline and I would sit on our couches with our laptops and simultaneously stream a movie.

I logged in just in time.

"Hey, Lina!" I said.

"Hi, Emma." Her face appeared on-screen with a big smile.

"So, what's it going to be tonight?" I asked.

"Well, I heard you haven't seen *It's a Wonderful Life*."

I slowly turned to my parents, my jaw dropping in outrage. They whistled and walked the other way.

"Okay. Fiiine," I said.

"Got your ramen popcorn ready?" she asked.

"Of course." I spun my fingers, and a bowl of ramen popcorn appeared on my lap.

Avangeline laughed. "I wish I could do that! Let's do it!"

We started watching, my eyes on both the movie and Avangeline's delighted smiles. And even though she wasn't next to me, even though I'd never really be normal, even though so much had changed and things would never be the same, I loved my life just as it was.

Acknowledgments

No book gets made without a lot of teamwork and a little bit of magic. Thank you to everyone at Bloomsbury Publishing for your help in getting Emma and Avangeline into the hands of readers. A special thank you to Camille Kellogg for first believing in this soft, magical story and for your invaluable assistance in shaping Emma's journey and bringing out the heart of this story. Extra thanks to Jennifer Bricking and Yelena Safronova for an outstanding cover. Thank you also to Donna Mark, Laura Phillips, Diane Aronson, Mary Kate Castellani, Sarah Shumway, Alona Fryman, Erica Chan, Ariana Abad, Briana Williams, Erica Barmash, Faye Bi, Phoebe Dyer, Beth Eller, Kathleen Morandini, Jennifer Choi, Andrew Nguyen, Nicholas Church, Valentina Rice and Daniel O'Connor for all of your hard work and special talents.

Thank you to Stephanie Kim for championing Emma. Thank you to my agent, Lauren Spieller, for just being fantastic and for guiding me through all of the changes in my career. Thank you to Krista Vitola, Jennifer Ung, and Lauren Abramo for helping me grow as an author.

I'm not sure where I'd be without finding the love of my life. Thank you John, for making even the good things even better like a pinch of salt in chocolate milk. Thank you for being the one to push me and the one to rest with. Thank you for being the reason I believe in love and kindness again.

Thank you to my fantastic writer friends, especially Karen McManus who never fails to amaze me. Thank you to Germany Jen for your insight and always looking out for me. Thank you to Julie Abe for reading the early draft and for inspiring me with your talent. Thank you to Jenn Dugan, Alexa Martin, Kiana Nyugen, June Tan, Caroline Richmond, Sabina Kahn, Sarah Suk, Emily Berge-Thielmann, and Sarah Hollowell for the writing sprints, coffees, and chats. Thank you to Dahlia Adler and Rachel Strolle for all your support for my books!

Thank you to all the educators, librarians, book bloggers, booktokers, bookstagrammers, and all reviewers who spent time in my worlds.

Thank you to my babies, my sunshine and heart. Your

pride in me does more for my heart than words can express. Thank you for being the reasons behind it all, but especially behind me writing middle grade. Thank you to my mom for supporting a different child and I'm sorry again for you not being on the bio for some weird reason. Thank you to Matt, Jessica, Susan, and Molly for your friendship and love. And thank you to anyone I left out. I will immediately and inevitably feel guilty and terrible for overlooking you.

Last but not least thank you, my readers, for taking this journey with me.